The Golden Orphans

Gary Raymond is a novelist, critic, editor and broadcaster. He is one of the founding editors of *Wales Arts Review*, and has been editor since 2014. His debut novel, *For Those Who Come After*, was published by Parthian in 2015. He is a widely published critic and cultural commentator, and is the presenter of BBC Radio Wales' *Arts Review* programme.

The Golden Orphans

Gary Raymond

Parthian, Cardigan SA43 1ED
www.parthianbooks.com
First published in 2018
© Gary Raymond 2018
ISBN 978-1-912109-13-5
Editor: Richard Davies
Cover design: www.theundercard.co.uk
Typeset by Elaine Sharples
Printed in EU by Pulsio SARL
Published with the financial support of the Welsh Books Council,
British Library Cataloguing in Publication Data
A cataloguing record for this book is available from the British Library.

To Bobby

One

Until the Russian turned up with his entourage, I was the only person at the funeral, and I had come two and a half thousand miles to be there. The priest, in his cassock and black hat, said that yes, he would have carried out the service alone if it had come to that, delivered the eulogy about a stranger to nothing but the heavy warm air and an audience of buried bodies. I didn't linger on my surprise at the turnout, saying only, "Is there really no-one else coming?" The priest carried with him the demeanour of a man more than halfway through a career that required little more than sympathetic nodding, and he said in good English, "Everything was arranged and paid for by Mr Prostakov, but that is all I know, I'm afraid." I took this in, took in the unfamiliar name, and perused the flat wilderness of the graveyard. I was just three hours on the island and I had seen little more than grasslands mixing in shades of tan and umber, the edges of villages emerging from diverging roadways, and isolated villas like discarded boxes flickering in the heat of the middle distance. My taxi driver had not spoken a word all the way from Larnaca, and I had lost my thoughts to the white noise of tyres on tarmac.

"Are you a relative of the deceased?" the priest asked.

I hesitated. I said that I was not, that he was an old friend, and that we had lost touch over the last few years. The priest nodded in the way he would have done no matter what my answer had been, and we walked together out to the plot at the far end of the graveyard.

"Who was it you said paid for the funeral?" I asked.

"Mr Prostakov."

"And why would he do that?"

"I believe he was Mr Benthem's employer."

I had questions, of course. Questions about Francis Benthem's death, about his life in the years since I had last seen him or heard from him – I had brought those questions with me on the flight. But I also had more immediate questions: what was the priest going to read? Had anybody else been informed? How had this afternoon all come about?

But I didn't ask any of them, immediate or otherwise. Through the warm air came a merciful breeze, and we both took positions at the graveside. There was Francis's coffin, the 'music box' as he used to refer to them: 'where the music stops'. He was in it, of course, and I hadn't really given much thought to the fact I would be standing so close to the cold remains of a man who taught me everything I knew about the path I had chosen in life, and in many ways had perhaps helped me choose that path. I had met him when he was a lecturer at St Martin's just over twenty years before, back when I was all piss and vinegar, a painter who felt he would change the world, just like almost everybody else who came through those doors. It was an institute of firebrands, from the student body all the way up through the faculty. Francis had a reputation for confrontation in the lecture hall, of deconstructing Young Turks, and was a member of the clique of the Fine Art faculty who still regularly made headlines with their work. My tilt to my moxie (as he would have put it) back then was to set fire to the establishment, of which I perceived Francis to be a member. He pointed out early on that it was an interesting tactic I had in hand, enrolling at St Martin's and deciding to set fire to the building I myself was now in. "Welcome to the establishment," he had said. "Set fire to what you want. It can take it."

There seemed something so small about that box. The priest

began his words but I didn't take them in. I hadn't noticed before, but a few yards away two gravediggers the colour of lead were sitting on a headstone smoking cigarettes, waiting for this odd little theatre to end so they could drop Francis into the ground. Francis had made a name for himself painting scenes like this just after the war, pulling shards of light onto mounds of morbid earth. He said to me once that the nineteen-forties was the only time when death was bigger than a conversation, it was a canvas rather than a scene; it was just there with all of us, like pissing and shitting, it didn't matter where you looked you always had one eye on it. Before that and after it, he said, death was not there until it happened, either to you or to someone you knew. I couldn't quite get over how much those two gravediggers looked like a Francis Benthem painting.

And that was how I caught a glance of the car making its way at some pace along the main road from Paralimni, the town the graveyard served. It left a gyre of dust in its wake as it silently came toward us, and the priest caught my distraction and he too looked out to the road and stopped speaking. The gravediggers looked back over their shoulders and hurriedly stubbed out their cigarettes.

I had come with few expectations other than hoping I might have my curiosities assuaged as to what had happened to my friend. But I had, I suppose, expected a large and emotional crowd to have surrounded me for the service. Even forgotten artists get one last swing at relevance when they are being buried, after all.

I looked across the hole at the priest, but it was clear from his face that he had no idea who this was.

When the car stopped – it was a long black Bentley with blacked out windows – it pulled up closer to the gravediggers than it did to Francis's coffin, and out stepped two young girls of late teens perhaps, both pretty with long blonde hair and sullen

3

expressions; what one might think of as well-practised mourning-gazes. Then came one man who looked around the same age as me – that is, touching forty, one side or the other – and finally an older man. The older man, coming last, had the build and swagger of authority; he was firm-footed and broad-chested, in all black – suit, shirt, tie, and shades – his bald head specked with a horseshoe of silver-white. He was thick-set, but had that intelligent look to him, an open brow and a jaw that one could imagine doing some athletic bouts of talking. The younger man held less of a presence; medium build and dark hair combed back behind his ears – he gathered the two girls together and seemed to say something to them as they waited by the car, and then they all put on dark glasses in a smooth choreographed movement. They were Russian I guessed on seeing them, or at least of that Russo-Slavic stock – they have a look, people from that part of the world, no less than people from other parts of the world have their look, and painters, like me, like Francis, have a trained eye for shoulder-width and cheekbones.

"Is this Mr Prostakov?" I said to the priest under my breath, but the priest shrugged.

The four of them walked up to the graveside; one of the girls had some flowers and she placed them onto Francis's coffin and then took a few steps back into the arms of the dark-haired man. It was impossible to tell if any of these four had as yet acknowledged the presence of either myself or the priest, until the tributes had been paid and flowers offered, and the older man raised an upturned palm to the priest in a pliant gesture to continue. When he was still, the older man had a hunched demeanour, and he curled his bottom lip and bobbed his head slightly as the priest spoke. It might have been approval, it might not. The younger man was more alert, glancing occasionally over his shoulder to the gravediggers, who had stood from their positions, their tools ready at their sides like sentries whose

4

sergeant had turned up. The girls aimed their shades toward the coffin respectfully, and did not move.

The priest continued on from his generic praise in English – he knew nothing of Francis after all, as he had admitted; not even that he had been a famous artist – and went on to read some verse from the Bible in Greek. The older Russian continued to bob his head and curl his lip. But at the first suggestion that the passage had been concluded he raised his hand once again, less passive this time, and flicked his wrist in the direction of the gravediggers, who applied an urgency I would not have imagined them capable of just fifteen minutes before. They came at a canter over to the plot and set about lowering Francis into the hole. As this went on, the priest went on too, in Greek, and the older man impatiently stood over the hole with a fistful of dirt. Another gesture from him, subtler, from behind his shades, and the others of his party likewise picked up dirt to cast down onto the coffin once lowered. And a strange thing: I too then found myself, from the other side of the hole, picking up some dirt having never done such a thing at any funeral before, even for my own family members.

The music box reached the floor of the grave and the diggers unhooked their tethers and stepped away. The old Russian stepped forward, muttered some words I couldn't catch – if they were even in English to be caught – and dropped his dirt.

With all that done, the younger man ushered the girls back in the direction of the car, but the older man stayed back and approached the priest with an outstretched hand. They shook and the Russian said some words in Greek that had the priest nodding with that sympathetic look on his face. And then the Russian pulled his shades an inch down the bridge of his nose and looked over the top of them directly at me. He had powerful blue eyes and it was just for a second, but everything seemed to slow down, drag out, and then he pushed them back up, closed his eyes off to me, and turned without a word to the Bentley.

I am not a reserved man as a rule – anybody back home would tell you that – and although Francis taught me the best home for my personality was the canvas, there were still those who preferred to keep me at arm's length. But I found conflicted in my chest the need to follow the Russian and talk to him, and the want to stay rooted by the graveside. I made eye contact with the priest, and now his demeanour did not seem quite so sympathetic, not quite so placid, and seemed something to do with taking me for a fool, and I wanted to say something unkind to him, or worse, put my forefinger to his shoulder. He seemed to read something of this in my face and the priest turned his attention away from me.

"So that was Mr Benthem's employer?" I said.

"I couldn't be certain," said the priest, as he walked back to the path. "He did not give his name. He just asked if everything was taken care of and I said that it was and he said that as long as we could leave it at that then he would be leaving."

"And that was that?"

"Well, yes. What more is there to say?"

It seemed there was no good place to begin on answering that question. I was angry, not just because Francis had been the recipient of a funeral so awash with the stuff of loneliness, but because I had come to it off the back of a letter requesting I attend, requesting, it turns out, I be the sole witness to this drudgery in the desert. And furthermore it had been a long time since I had housed the energy for a run-around the likes of which Francis Benthem enjoyed, and I knew the look of a man who could not be trusted as effortlessly as I knew how to spot a Russian. Grifters, gangsters and wide-boys had been as common as furniture when I had started out in Soho, and that kind hung around the fringes of the big art scene the whole time I had had my foot in the door – from the late 'eighties – since I had met Francis. There would always be some aspirational miscreant

6

looking to turn an artist into a fraudster, offering to introduce you to a 'friend of his' who needed a Titian for a 'private buyer'. I wagered Prostakov had a house filled with rip-offs looking down on Siberian tiger hide rugs. I was angry at how seedy Francis's ending had been, with little evidence other than that created in my own imagination. I was angry I had gone all the way out there to begin with, to see it, to have *this* Francis now the one of my memory, and not the dashing, darting swashbuckler I had known back in London.

Two

There is no one easier to lie to than the person standing the opposite side of a bar to you, and yet, for me at least, a barkeep always seems to bring out a frictionless truth. The day after Francis was buried, I had walked around Paralimni, a characterless circular town of mall-shops and clean pavements, until I made myself comfortable on a barstool in a place looking out across the town square. The barmaid asked me how long I would be on the island, and I said, without even thinking, "I honestly couldn't say at this point."

"So you are not on a holiday?" she said.

"I wouldn't call it that, no," I said. "I came to say goodbye to an old friend."

She was wiping glasses, then cleaning surfaces, then dicing lemons as we spoke, and there was nobody else at the bar, just another waiter relaying drinks orders from scattered people at a few tables on the veranda.

"And what is it you do for a living?" she asked. I said I was an artist, a painter, and she smiled in a lackadaisical way, not too impressed, but something more engaged perhaps than if I had said I was an insurance broker or a structural engineer. The usual set of questions came next, the ones that break down the defences of that original answer – *What kind of artist? What do you paint? What's the most you've ever sold a painting for?*

And it's the last answer that always sticks in the craw. The most? A great deal. The only thing that matters is that it was a long time ago. It matters even more I should probably have got double for it. But the dominant point is that I had not sold a painting in nearly four years. "I think I have been holding out for a miracle, and unfortunately it was my friend who was the guy who usually provided them," I said.

"Your friend could not help you?"

"Not this time."

We both smiled, different smiles that may have looked on the same page to a casual observer – both half-formed and delivered with something of a shrug. I was picking apart a cardboard beermat with my fingers, and she was trying to console me the best she could with the advised distance of a professional counsellor.

"This is a good place to figure things out," she said.

"This bar?" I said, looking around the place.

"Cyprus," she said with that smile again. "Nobody is going to rush you to any conclusions here. There is a *Cypriot* way of things."

"And what way is that?" I said.

But she just shrugged, half-smiled and half-turned away from me. She could have only meant that the Cypriot way, as she called it, is the way that things naturally come to fruition. The shrug, the smile, the turn of the hips, this wasn't mysticism, it was the extreme relaxation of Mediterranean pragmatism. That and the unmistakeable grit of island air; it calms the most frayed of nerves.

I ordered another beer, but the serving of it was slowed by a noise outside. It was the noise of a gathering crowd, and when I looked back to the barmaid she was rolling her eyes at me.

"This happens sometimes this time of year," she said. "It's the heat."

I got up from my stool and walked over to the veranda to see the crowd forming at the edge of the square just a few yards from the bar. Twenty people or so, coming down from the neighbouring mezze places and the pool hall, and in the centre were two young Cypriot-looking men stripped to the waist. I found myself stepping out onto the veranda, but still not yet out onto the street, as the two young men raised their fists to guard and began circling each other. The barmaid was at my shoulder.

"A street fight?" I said. "That can't be good for the tourist trade."

"It's not," she said. "Can you watch the bar for a second while I go and get my boss."

I said I would, and no sooner had she disappeared off the forecourt than the fight began. The first few punches were swings that turned over nothing but air, but these were well-built guys in their early twenties, athletic, and they could clearly both box – I prepared for the show to get a little brutal. The first punch shaved the one guy's cheek, and I winced knowing if it had connected fully it would have likely knocked him into the middle of next week. More swipes at the air but these were good punches, it was just the ducks and dives were better. I'd seen a fair few brawls in my time – more than my fair few in actual fact – but this had a brutal poise, an artistry not often seen at chucking out time on Berwick Street. The crowd that had gathered did not holler and bay for blood, but they watched intently, offered a few calls of encouragement. I could not help but feel they were there mostly to make sure nothing got out of hand.

The pace picked up as the two broke into a sweat in the midday heat, and the one man who had had his punches blocked up high was already showing bruises on his forearms. A few body blows, which landed from both, were taken courageously and then the wrestling ensued and the one man lunged and threw the other back into the middle of the road, the crowd parting as he went. I saw then at the door of the pool hall a very pretty young dark-skinned girl standing alone watching with her hand nervously up to her mouth, and I wondered if this was the cause of the dispute.

10

It seemed somewhat honourable, and more so by the minute, the way the two men had squared up, the way they had stripped to the waist, the way they boxed rather than brawled – at the outset, at least – and now I had decided it was for the honour of a beautiful young girl. Two weeks before I had been drunk in south London and watched as a woman pushed her boyfriend into a pile of bin bags outside the pub they had both just been kicked out of, before going on to attack him with her shoe as he tried to heave himself up from the spilled kebabs and vomit splashes.

I was looking across to this girl as I felt someone go past me and then became aware that the barmaid was back at my shoulder. The tank of a man who had walked from the bar into the square was "the boss", the owner of the bar I was drinking in, and the entire atmosphere seemed to change. It took perhaps a moment to realise that it was not changing darker, for the worse, but was actually about to signal the end of the fight. The boss was an impressive looking gentleman, perhaps around his forty-year mark, and built like a battle ram, with his neck down into his enormous shoulders and his prominent forehead out in front of him as he walked. This was a man who knew the inside of a gym intimately, but beyond that he commanded the space around him and I couldn't put my finger on how or why he had that command. The crowd split and some backed off quickly, and the two opponents dropped their guards the moment they saw him. Immediately they looked younger next to him, maybe eighteen or nineteen, and their heads sunk. The boss brought his forefinger up like a baton and began a tirade of Cypriot Greek that was my introduction to the language as martial art. He pointed at them, and then at each of the businesses along the square front in turn. I don't know what he said, although the theme was clear. They both meekly nodded but he went on, and then the pretty girl cantered over and began to apologise in the space left by her suitors' silences. Finally, the boss clipped the one guy around the back of the head like he was a misbehaving schoolboy, and when the other objected he raised a fist and that was the end of that. Both fighters clearly could not afford for things to go any further and they pleaded for forgiveness. The girl was close to tears. It was not clear by the time it all ended which of the two had won her heart, but at least both of their hearts continued to beat.

The boss marched back into the bar and on seeing me – his anger had clearly blinded him to my presence on his way out into the square – he changed course through the tables and came up to me. His face altered as he did so, from stern and purposeful to relaxed and friendly.

"Sir," he said as he walked up, "please accept my apology for what you just had to witness in the street. I will tell Veronika to pour you a drink on the house."

His voice was soft and I was thrown by it a little. It was far from the intimidating ferocity I had just witnessed out in the square. I nodded in acceptance of the offer – never turn down hospitality, I thought – and he was gone off again through the kitchen swing doors, gesturing to the barmaid his instruction en route.

"That was quite a thing," I said back at the bar.

The barmaid nodded as she tiptoed up to the tall chrome beer tap and poured me my third beer. "People do as they're told for Furkan," she said.

I wanted to talk more about what had just happened, I was curious about Furkan and about the characters out in the square, but I caught something out of the corner of my eye. A long Bentley with blacked out windows had pulled up outside the bar.

I did not recognise the man who stepped out of it but I knew straight away he was looking for me. It was safe to assume he was the unseen driver of the car at the funeral the day before. I was nervous; he was a big man, hired for his physique, I guessed, as much as for any administrative role he may have been asked to fill in whatever business Mr Prostakov was running. And this man spoke with the low gravel-inflected tones of the stereotype muscle, his voice wet with Russian undulations.

"Are you the painter Mr Benthem sent for in his will?" he said once up to me. I tried to steady my hands by holding on firmly to the beer glass and I looked over the top of it at him as I drank slowly. "You are the painter?" he repeated. I nodded. "Mr Prostakov wishes to extend you an invitation to his home. He regrets to say he is busy today, but would like you to come here..." he handed me a card from his jacket pocket; "... at noon tomorrow."

I took the card. The address I glanced at meant nothing to me. "What does Mr Prostakov want with me?" I said.

The man looked faintly surprised. "He has something for you."

And he dipped his head politely to the barmaid and turned and left, the Bentley pulling off with idiosyncratic grace.

It took a few minutes to compose myself, before turning to the barmaid and saying, "Can you tell me anything about Mr Prostakov?"

But she could not. Cyprus is crawling with Russians, she said. And they bring with them a lot of Russian girls, so young women like her tend to be left alone. It was not an exchange that left me feeling particularly positive.

The barmaid, Veronika, and I did not really talk again that afternoon, although I stayed for two or three more beers, before getting a taxi down to Nisi Beach where I slept hunched against a rock for a few hours and woke up feeling extremely unwell – a mixture of the acidic Cypriot lager and the fact I had fallen asleep in the shade and awoken in the full glare of the sun. I walked up to the main street and ordered a plate of pork chops in a sports bar before getting a taxi back to the hotel in Protaras I had quickly checked into just a few hours before the funeral. It was an austere and unwelcoming place, gleaming with tile work, a lobby with only vending machines for furniture, an out-of-order elevator, and a staircase prohibitive with the hot heavy stench of stale air and sweat. The sun had dipped but the heat had stayed, and I was not feeling much better. I made the mistake of making the promised phone call back home near the breeze of my balcony open to the evening buzz of Protaras' family vacationers filling the streets in search of their evening meals.

"I think I may have got some sunstroke this afternoon," I said to Clare who would have been both waiting for my call and assuming it would be late. I knew immediately almost everything I would attempt to say would be ammunition for her. I had left abruptly, without much of a plan of how to circumnavigate various familiar-yet-new financial problems I had brought down upon us.

"I am glad you're finding time to hit the beach," she said. "Also glad you find time to call. It sounds like you booked in to party central."

"No, actually. It's the family resort. Just the wrong time of day. It's normally very quiet so far as I understand it."

"Okay."

"I'm serious. I didn't come here to escape, Clare."

"And yet escape you did. As you tend to do. I had no intention of stopping you going to your friend's funeral, but you could have gone about it differently."

"The story of my life," I said with an unintentional sigh.

"You can turn this into a series of meaningless idioms if you like, but tomorrow I have to phone my father to borrow some money, and you know what he's going to say? He's going to say what the fuck are you still doing with that dickhead?"

"And what are you going to say?" I said.

"Well, let's just say I didn't used to have to think about an answer in advance."

That was the kind of conversation the two of us were getting used to. The sad thing was we both knew Clare wanted me back in London because I had a duty to clear up my own mess, and not because she missed me or wanted to see me. It would have been a rare thing indeed in my experience to have been in a relationship not drowning in clutter. I guess that's what had happened even between Francis and me. He had served his time at St Martin's and had bailed me out himself enough times, but when he left, without much fanfare it must be said, it felt like the cutting of a cord, as if he had had enough of the clutter – not just with me, but with all of the kind of life we knew back then. And it was ten years, or thereabouts, between him leaving and me receiving that letter from a solicitor in Larnaca, informing me of his death, with a return flight booked and paid for. All sorted. I'd figured he just wanted me to say goodbye.

Clare did ask about the funeral, of a man she never knew and a man I had barely mentioned in the years of our relationship; but she believed me when I said this stranger had been like a father to me, and she asked how the funeral had gone, and, for some reason, I had lied about it almost entirely. I said it was well-attended and I had been pleasantly surprised to see some old friends there: "Y'know how funerals are; they bring all sorts of things out of the past and bring them right up to your nose."

"Some old friends?" she said.

"Not girlfriends," I said.

"I didn't mean that, you wanker."

I wasn't sure if we were joking with each other or not.

"But it does mean I'd like to stay a few more days," I said. "Who knows what might come out of it. There are a few dealers here, and some friends of Francis's from way back who might have some connections for me. It's networking, y'know? Just hold off calling your dad until the end of the week, will you?"

Clare sighed deeply.

"I have two auditions tomorrow, so I'll call him Friday," she said. The tone was delivered so there could be no doubt this was a stay of execution and not a relaxing of Clare's feelings toward me at that time. The conversation had exhausted itself, and had tapered off to something much more demeaning than the usual combat – it was being dismissed now.

"Was there anything else?" Clare said.

Regardless of her anger, and how much I had been dreading calling her, I had enjoyed hearing her voice. It was always so steady and confident and even as she was reprimanding me I felt I was being done some good rather than just being reminded of my failings. She had wanted to tell me she was cancelling the lease on my studio, and that if I didn't take the art teaching position at the tertiary college next term she would leave me. She wanted to tell me it was not my talent that was driving us out of our home, but my personality. At the lowest, loudest points in recent months she had said all of these things, and much more besides. I looked out over the family vacationers wandering the wide streets of Protaras, down to the waterfront, took in a lungful of warm salty air, and felt my head begin to spin. I put my feet up on the balcony and tilted my head back in the chair, knowing full well I would regret sleeping out there, inviting as I was the external noises to infiltrate whatever lucid drunken dreams were coming my way.

Three

Mid-morning, a taxi took me through bright refreshing fields of yellow hyacinths to the Russian's house in the wilderness land outside of Sotira. For an island you can cover in half a day, these open flats gave an impression of vastness. It was something to do with the colour – that sandy scrub – but also the clean blueness of the sky, and the lowness of it. There was a place in those plains where neighbouring villas became dots on the horizon, and then trees began to sprout up in the south like bushels of broccoli from the scrubland. We passed a few driveways that were not the routes to farmhouses, but to the isolated homes of people with money, and the further south we went the taller the trees became, the greater the distance between driveways.

My driver seemed to cool off a bit – he had been quite talkative despite his lack of English. Something about the Russian seemed to dry his mouth. The drive to Prostakov's house was long but not at all hidden from the road – it was cleared of trees and unfenced – but then the road sunk into a strange valley and up past a concealing tump of earth.

It was a two-storey villa with colonnades and a welcoming gravel square complete with dry fountain out in front of the entrance. At the top of the steps was the man who had come to see me the day before at the bar, and as the taxi pulled up he came down to open the door for me. He also paid the driver and waved him on his way.

"Mr Prostakov is waiting," he said and ushered me up the steps and into the house. Before entering, I could see that the house went back much further than it first appeared, and there were several annexes around the side of it leading off into the shallow valley; there was a pool and a garage, the doors of which were raised. The radiators of several expensive, some vintage, cars could be seen hidden away in there. I thought I could see a few figures down by the pool, distant and silhouetted against the sparkle of the sun reflecting off the marble of the patio.

Inside the house, two rather vulgar and enormous sculptures of Samurai warriors in sentry pose stood either side of the gilded looping staircase. And I noticed almost immediately the Francis Benthem above the bureau. A stormy fishing harbour somewhere, most likely, off the Yorkshire coast – he had composed a series of them in the late 'seventies. The architecture, as far as my eye could pick out, was an off-putting mix of Italianate and Moorish. It all gave the place a feeling more of a museum or even a warehouse for an auctioneer. From the top of the stairs Prostakov came into my eye-line, and his gruff purposeful stride brought with it an emergent smile, which I had not been expecting given his demeanour at the funeral.

"I had no idea who you were when I saw you yesterday," he said, and held his hand out to me.

"That makes two of us," I said and although being firmly on the back foot I shook his hand.

"Ah, yes, but I know who you are," he said. "I even know your work."

"I can see you are a collector." I said it with the words almost trapped between my teeth, because I was being sarcastic, but I had no intention of being rude. The perfect example of nature battling against nous.

He recognised this tension, I could tell easily.

"But still it is *something* to have heard of you, is it not?" he said.

"I am flattered, Mr Prostakov; don't take me the wrong way."

"Ah, I am, for the main part, just fucking with you." And he let out a big hollow laugh that flipped his head back to get out. "I mean I had heard of you, and I *do* know your work; but I owe most of my education to Francis."

"I see."

"Yes, you see. Our mutual friend." And he slapped me, not too lightly, with the back of his hand across the shoulder.

At close quarters, Prostakov – or Illarion: he would insist I call him Illie – had an indefinable warmth to him; perhaps it was something in his eyes, or the way the eyes clamped on you. They were quite beautiful, with long lashes and a citrusy light that came through the iris. His rugged face was dimpled all across the jaw with shoals of pockmarks.

"I have to admit to you," he went on, leading me into a sitting room off to the left where he began mixing drinks at a small cabinet, "that I also know you because nobody else was invited to the funeral, and it was my solicitor who executed Francis's will. So in a way it was I who sent for you."

He did not ask me if I wanted a drink or what I might have wanted, but he continued to pour some clear spirit and various mixers into a shaker, and when he carefully tipped the concoction out into two Manhattan glasses it was a bold shade of green. He handed me one and when he noticed my face, which must have been as mixed as the drink, he chinked my glass with the rim of his and said, "My own recipe. We call it, Illie's Green Slime." And he burst out laughing, again with that flip top action. When I tasted it, staring the Russian in the eyes as I did so, my head almost made a similar action, although I was not inclined to laugh along with it.

"You drink these at lunchtime often?" I said, choking back.

"You think I made it to my age drinking *this* every day?" he said, taking the glass out of my hand and putting both drinks unfinished back on the bar. "Come on, let's see if there is some fresh lemonade in the kitchen, and then I'll take you out to the studio."

I followed him again, this energetic, curious figure.

The place felt lonely. I had seen somebody down by the pool, maybe a couple of people, and I had been shown in by his driver, but there was no sense that there was anybody else around now. He walked me back through the hallway past the staircase – I took a shy glimpse of the towering Samurais – and through to the anaesthetic surfaces of the kitchen.

"So you were a student of Francis?" he said with his head in one of the industrial chrome refrigerators.

"Quite some time ago," I said. It was a house that deserved staff, and yet there was no sign of them or signs of where they might have been.

"But you have made a name for yourself since then, no?" He backed out from the fridge precariously carrying a jug of pale yellow liquid. "Francis wouldn't have put in his will for you to come here if he didn't think highly of your work."

"I honestly couldn't say what his motivations were, Mr Prostakov."

This seemed to catch him off stride a little. "Ah, yes, I understand, of course. And make sure you call me Illarion. Illie; call me Illie." And he stopped his search for glasses into which to pour the cloudy lemonade. "I should have been clear from the beginning. There is always so much to remember." He walked over to a door that seemed to lead back outside and he said, "Francis's belongings."

"What about them?" I said.

"Come. I'll show you." And he opened the door and went out into the heat of the day.

My footing was off by now – I had come expecting a hard encounter, one with an intimidating Russian who would explain something to me about Francis and perhaps I would leave somewhat less of a man than I had arrived, but I had taken solace in the fact I was expected to make my own way out there, and had not been either fetched or tumbled into the back of that Bentley against my will. But still, I expected to be glad to be leaving. It was curiosity that had got me there in the first place, and my mind had been on the ten-year absence of Francis perhaps more than it had been on any potential danger from the Russians. But here was an altogether unexpected environment. There was something of the eccentric in his castle about Illarion Prostakov.

Outside in the open air, however, he seemed to grow in stature. His chest barrelled out and his shoulders broadened, and I noticed for the first time that in black slacks and a skin-tight black T-shirt he showed clear definition of his excellent physique. I had little doubt this old man could pack a punch.

"Walk with me down to the studio," he said.

We took a path that stretched along a ridge looking down to the pool and pool house – there was nobody there now – and then over to the foot of the opposite side of that shallow valley wall. And as I looked down from the ridge to the other side from the pool I could see what appeared to be – from its unusually straight edges and eerie isolation – a man-made woodland. It was quite dense in the centre, but out at the edges the trees were still only half-grown, and they became smaller as the edges thinned out. And then I saw where we were headed.

"This was Francis's studio," Prostakov said. He walked at a glide, his nose raised to the breeze, his aviators now on, his face serious, and he seemed more the intimidating figure I had encountered at the funeral.

"He worked here?" I said, unable to hide my surprise. Francis Benthem's studio was a converted brick water tower in the middle of scrubland a good few hundred yards away from any other structure on the estate.

Prostakov gestured that I was correct. The picture was now becoming clearer, less blurred, although I still could not figure

21

out any of the details. If I had ever thought Francis had given up painting, I had been wrong. He had left Britain, left St Martin's, concerned about his finances. I remember he had said to me that his retirement could be in jeopardy, but that he was determined to see out life as a victor. Too many of his contemporaries had sparked in the midpoint and fizzled out to destitution by the end, and he refused to go the same way. What brought him to Cyprus? The Mediterranean retirement was always his romantic vision of his final years, painting his late-phase masterpieces overlooking a glass-blue cove. It seems it had not been far from the truth.

The studio was not simply a workspace, it was Francis Benthem's home. The building was two storeys, a circular tower with several balconies looking out to east and west – over the man-made wood, and back over toward the house. The tower was really one room, the ground floor studio with a mezzanine that housed Francis's bed and shower facilities. At the doorway I knew it was immediately Francis's place – his fingerprints were everywhere, in the form of shredded newspapers, paint-smeared jam jars spouting threadbare brushes, slashed canvases, the tools for canvas-mounting, and pinboards decking the walls covered in cuttings from Cypriot and English newspapers. This was how Francis had always worked, how he had always nested. It was as if he was still there. I could smell his smell.

Afterwards it occurred to me that Prostakov had given me a moment to come to terms with the atmosphere of the room – it wasn't so much that I felt emotional, which I did, but rather that these were long-distant sentiments, long-forgotten details of a past friendship that had become, in my mind, broad and dense. Francis used to say that a painting offers an electronic impulse of a vision, and that is what he had become to me, a story that would jolt me from afar.

"So, everything in here is belonging to Francis," Porstakov said. "And he says in his will that seeing as he has no children and his wife died many years ago that he wanted you to have claim."

I looked around the room. There was a treasure trove of objects for admirers of Francis Benthem, but little of intrinsic value. I thought of Clare back home.

"He worked for you?" I said.

"Nothing quite as vulgar as that." Prostakov held up his hands in front of a cheeky half-smile. He had pushed his shades up onto his velvety cranium. "We had a mutual arrangement."

I did not want to press it, but at the same time something did not feel right. I walked around the room, examining casually the bric-a-brac of Francis's working space.

"And all this is for me?"

"It is not much perhaps, but it is what he wanted for you."

"You were close?"

"We became friends," said Prostakov.

"What exactly did he do for you? Can you tell me that?"

"Tell you? Why could I *not* tell you?"

He was speaking lightly, although I could see in him a figure who had delivered countless threats in his life; it was just under the surface, perhaps even his natural pose.

"Illie…" It was the first time I had attempted to obey his invitation to address him so familiarly, and it made no ruffle in him, so I went on. "This is an uncommon set-up. You understand?"

He sucked his teeth, crossed his arms, and leaned back on the doorframe. "You want to know what he did? What he did for all this?"

I continued to go through the things in the room cursorily.

"It has been many years since I heard anything about Francis," I said. "And then I am notified of his death and funeral and I get here and I am summoned by a man, a man with the appearance of a powerful man, and he tells me that Francis has spent all these years painting for him, and now he is dead and I can have all these things. That brings up more questions than answers."

Prostakov rubbed his rough hands across his neck and looked me up and down. I could not tell if he was angry or not. But then he went on: "He worked for me for the last three years or so. I met him just after I moved to Cyprus. I came across his work in a gallery in Napa."

"Francis was exhibiting here?"

"He was. And I came upon his work and I saw that he could do a very good job for me and so we became friends. He was living in some very unsatisfactory conditions – for a painter, you understand – not far from the barracks – how he ever got any painting done there I will never guess – but he did, and it brought us together. We both liked expensive booze. Some great friendships of mine have started with that connection. But I built this for him."

"You built it for him?"

"Well, it was a mill, or water tower, or something like that. I cannot really say. But it did not take much from some local craftsmen to turn it into a spot for Francis to set up." Prostakov peered up to the mezzanine. "Francis really loved it here, I think."

I realised I had been pushing, and it was inappropriate and ill-mannered. There was even a chance I had been letting my imagination run away with me. There was nothing to confirm Prostakov was anything other than a retired businessman of some sort. He had a hard version of himself, worn on the exterior, as all successful people do by this last act of their lives, and I had mistaken it for some kind of roguishness. But inside of that was the same soft truth that had always been there – a need for friendships and most likely love, and an enjoyment of indulgences. I felt a little silly, and slightly ashamed.

I looked around the room once more, figuring to see if there was enough there to clear a debt or two, but I quickly doubted the potential. It didn't matter anyhow – it was unlikely I could have brought myself to pillage Francis's belongings in that way. Desperation had its limits, even for me.

"How about I give you some time here alone?" Prostakov said.

I nodded with solemn reflection.

I watched him make his way back along the ridge from one of the balconies. I admired that purposeful walk of his along the parapet between the swimming pool and the woodland. He was not a man I would have ever envisaged making any kind of connection with Francis – not the Francis I knew back then, anyway. Francis liked to surround himself with thinkers – or at least in my case, young idiots who showed potential for thinking. What was it he saw in Illie Prostakov? Perhaps there was nothing to it other than a man finding space for the twilight years of his life. And quite a beautiful place he had found too. I walked around the tower, examining it much more closely now I was unobserved. And there were some curiosities amongst the clutter.

A stack of sketches, for example, of a child's swing, in various states of completion; in charcoal, pencil, watercolour, and on various weaves of paper and parchment, some very stiff – I lifted them like boards – and others on recycled pads. The newspaper clippings on the walls, unusually, had little to do with art, but were news stories that seemed to bear no superficial connection. And there were personal items – items that slowed me in my tracks, such as his watch and his pipe. It was often commented on that Francis never smoked his pipe, that he wore it between his teeth for effect, that he pointed with it as he lectured (both in the lecture hall and in the pub) as if it was a baton; but he told me that he had once smoked it – indeed after the war and all the way through the 'sixties he had smoked it, but when he gave up at the request of his beloved wife he could not bear to let go of it. I picked it up, sniffed at it, and it seemed in these last years he had returned to lighting it.

I spent quite some time in that tower, sat in Francis's chair, holding his brushes, looking through his untouched canvases. There was a lack of works-in-progress, a lack of works completed.

"You look comfortable." Prostakov was back at the door with a smile on his face.

I looked up at him from the low wingback chair that had all the hallmarks of Francis's favoured spot – his pipe paraphernalia and dirty brandy glass were within arm's-reach from where he could admire and deconstruct a work in progress.

"There is much I don't understand," I said.

"This is natural," said Illie. "This was a man you held a great fondness for, but he had found another life for himself, and you know nothing of it."

"It's an odd feeling I have."

"Tell me."

"I have questions, and I feel I can ask you them, but at the same time I feel like I am not entirely safe here."

I was being more honest than I would have liked.

"Ask me a question, and we'll see how safe you are."

I thought for a second.

"How did Francis die?"

"How do any of us die who see this thing through to the end? His heart gave out. He had fulfilled his promises to God and his loved ones. He was done."

"He just *died*?"

"Right here. At this doorway. I found him early one morning. He had come to the door to maybe catch his breath but sadly it was no good."

I felt Francis very close at that moment, and I stared at the floor where Illie had found him.

"What is it Francis was doing here?" I said.

"Working," Illie said nonchalantly.

"But doing what?"

26

"Painting."

"And?" I said, pushing my luck.

"He painted on demand," Illie said. "You could say that I have insatiable visual desires. And Francis satiated those desires."

It was a difficult answer to hear, but at least it was progress. Francis had made a life for himself creating works of art for an eccentric Russian in the wilds of Cyprus. It was far removed from the urban firebrand that the art world, and I, had known and admired.

"Are you going to be taking his things?" Illie said, breaking the silence between us.

I gave it a few moments' thought but then said, "I don't think so. I'll take his watch, as a memento." I held it up by the strap. "But nothing else."

He nodded conciliatorily and stepped further into the tower. "Come with me," he said.

I followed him up to the mezzanine, where Francis's bed lay neatly made, and onto the balcony looking out over the valley. I don't think I had ever seen a clearer view, as if the air was so fine and the day so warm it had improved my eyesight by several points.

"I brought Francis here," Illie said, "and I told him I would make this place exactly what he wanted if he agreed to help me. No complications, no obligations. As long as he was happy to be here."

I thought about this speech, took in the beautiful view, imagined my brush rippling through the colours of the white-blue horizon.

"I am grateful that you could do this for him in the last years of his life," I said eventually. "I loved him, I don't mind saying. When it comes to art, to my craft, he was a father to me. And even though we lost touch, I am grateful to you for giving him all this."

Prostakov nodded, and we stood side-by-side looking out over the wood and off toward the coastline.

"I am still in need," he said after a while.

I was not sure what he meant.

"With Francis gone," he went on, "I am once again in need of an artist of great vision and talent to work for me."

I said nothing.

"Would you enjoy these surroundings?" he said.

"You're offering me a job?"

"I think it is a shame you belittle what I am offering," he said. "If you want to think of this as a job offer..." and he slowly waved his hand across the view, as if colouring a monochrome as he went.

It was the last thing I had been expecting. And I continued to think of it as a trick, examining Prostakov's face for signs of the prank.

"I didn't just invite you here to hand over all that rubbish," he said. "And I am certain Francis did not send for you just to clear out his rooms. I believe he meant to bring us together."

It was at this point things were beginning to make sense to me, although I still had no idea where the real dangers lay. I had been lured here, by a dead man.

"I can't help you," I said.

"But you're thinking about it," he said with a wry smile.

"There is nothing to think about. I cannot stay here. I have to get home. I have things I need to attend to."

"Francis said you were never good with money. Is that what you need to get back to? A job you hate to pay debts you have no enthusiasm to repay?"

"No. I have an apartment and a girlfriend who needs me."

"I'll give you ten thousand euros."

He said this snappily, almost cutting me off. I was not quite sure how to respond to an offer like that, having never in my life had one before.

28

"You're offering me ten thousand euros?" I said, almost just to fill the silence.

"At first. If it helps."

"At first?"

"The arrangement I had with Francis was that he would let me know if he needed money, of any amount, for anything. And I would give it to him."

"But that's like an allowance, not like a wage at all."

Prostakov nodded in agreement. "Perhaps our arrangement would be different to that. I understand it might not work for everyone."

"So, we're negotiating now?" I said.

Prostakov smiled and dipped his eyes to me. "You are a funny man," he said. "I understand instantaneously what Francis saw in you." He put his arm around me – it was thick and cold. "Listen to me," he said, "you go back to your hotel and have a nice meal and nice drink and think about it. Call your girlfriend and see if she wants you to either go home so the two of you can fight about being penniless, or whether she'd like you to stay out here a while and I will make all those vultures fly away. Because these people are vultures, aren't they? And you know what vultures do, don't you? They wait for you to die before they come down for their fill. Not a moment too soon. None of them are hoping you recover."

He spoke as if he knew more about my financial situation than he was letting on, and that the revelation Francis had picked me to fill his vacated seat in this tower was just the tip of the iceberg.

"I don't want to sound overly dramatic," Illie went on, walking me back down from the mezzanine and out the tower door, "but I am offering you a once in a lifetime opportunity here."

"And I appreciate it," I found myself saying.

I told him I would think it over, without asking any more about

29

what the job really involved and what would be expected of me. When I did bring it up on the walk back to the house he would just shrug and laugh and say, "I need you to paint – what more is there to say?"

Back at the house he offered me one drink – he said it was a Russian tradition when an offer had been made, for the two sides of the bargain to share a drink and then share another when a decision had been made. We stood in the barroom I had been shown into and given the Green Slime on my arrival and he handed me the shot of potato vodka in a thimble glass much taller than those which house a single measure. We saluted and necked them both – it went down like ice-cold, creamy gasoline and I could not hold in my grimace. Prostakov laughed and slapped me across the shoulder.

"Next time you come I will cook and we will enjoy some cigars," he said.

"You cook?" I said.

"I enjoy it," he said.

"It's not that. I just thought you'd have a chef or something? It's a big old house. I saw some people down by the pool when I arrived. Is that your family?"

Prostakov shook his head and took the empty shot glass from my hand.

"Nobody here but me," he said. "And Viktor, who you met yesterday."

I thought of pressing it, asking who the man and girls were at the funeral, and I could see in his eyes he was waiting for that line, but instead I said, "I must have been mistaken. A trick of the light."

"Tricky light," he said and sniggered. "I would offer you another drink – I find you good company – but it would spoil the bargain we just entered into."

"The bargain?"

30

"That you would think about my offer," he said.

He had me driven back to Protaras by his man, Viktor, who kept an uncomfortable silence from the driver seat, and offered up very little welcome when I asked him about the people I had seen by the pool. He too said I must have been mistaken.

Four

It was not such an easy thing to just say yes to Illie Prostakov. The money would have changed everything with Clare, blown debtors off my back. Part of me wanted to tell her, wanted to call her up immediately and say that everything was going to be okay, just for the price of a little intrigue and sacrifice. *What sacrifice?* she might well have said. And thinking of the tower and the idyllic life I may have been stepping into, I would have found it difficult to argue her down from that point. But it was the best of both worlds for us, wasn't it? I had stepped up, cleared the mess, and had also given her space I knew she needed. Paying up and staying away was the optimum scenario; coming home empty handed would have been the nadir.

But it was not just about Clare, who, with this offer on the table, I could once again view without cloud. If I acted afraid of her, it was a fear of being thought of badly by her that instilled that fear. It was the sadness of losing respect.

At Prostakov's estate I had entered a wonderland. Nothing was quite as it seemed and every minor instruction had at its base a riddle. I still did not know who Prostakov was, or what his real relationship with Francis had been. That place he lived at was an isolated dream, and not an ideal, but an unsteady realm where truth seemed to bend in and out of focus.

I cut Viktor short and asked him to drop me at the bar in Parilimni where I had made myself comfortable after the funeral. At least where my drinking was concerned, I was a creature of quickly formed habit.

The barmaid, Veronika, was not there, but a young man tended bar in her place. There had been something circling me that she had said the day before and I hadn't even noticed it was there. She had said something about Russians and their girls, or that they always brought their girls with them, or something along those lines. And now the thought of the people by Prostakov's pool would not let go, and somewhere the two unshakeable notions met and created a whole new angle of suspicion.

"Do you know anything about Illarion Prostakov?" I said to the barman. He was not as friendly as Veronika, and he just shrugged at me. "A Russian," I said, as if the name I'd just given sounded anything else. "Is your boss here?" This seemed to worry the man, as if I was angling to make a complaint, and he began to plead that he knew a few Russians but not always by name and that they tended to keep to themselves, to their own bars and clubs and this place was *one hundred percent Cypriot*. He said it proudly, but also kind of spat it at me, as if my suggestion that it had been otherwise – which I hadn't made – was a great affront.

"I just wanted to speak to your boss," I muttered at him. "No need to make a big deal out of it."

Everything calmed down and I leaned back on my stool and gazed out of the bar toward the square hoping averting eye contact would diffuse the situation. But he clicked his fingers at me.

"I am sorry, sir," he was saying, and he was pouring another beer. "Please, sir, I am sorry. I was very rude, please accept this beer."

"It's not a problem," I said, but he insisted.

"My English," he said and shook his head. "I thought you were looking to make trouble."

"No trouble," I said. "I met your boss yesterday, and Veronika. I thought they could help me out with a few things."

He put the beer in front of me on a paper tab.

"My boss, he will be in Napa tonight," he said. "You can find him in Napa."

"A night off?"

The man laughed. "Oh, no, Furkan never has a night off. He has many businesses. Tonight he is in Napa."

"And Veronika?"

He shrugged.

"Where in Napa will I find Furkan?"

"Impossible to say. He has four bars. Ask around."

"Napa has a bit of a reputation," I said. He looked as though he only half understood. "It is a lively place," I said.

He laughed his detached condescending laugh.

"Oh yes," he said.

"Will I be okay down there? I am not as young as I used to be."

That laugh again.

"Napa is Napa, you know?"

Napa is Napa. Indeed it was.

It was early evening when I reached the main drag by taxi, and was met by a regiment of young girls handing out flyers for the array of bars and clubs along the strip. Like a poor swimmer getting into ice cold water, I went for the first rock I could hold on to and ducked into a sports bar at the top end and ordered a Cypriot lager. I didn't really notice, but the barman was an older guy, who on speaking offered up his thick Irish brogue. He cocked a look at me and said, "How's about a Guinness there, fella?"

I thought it was some kind of trite promotion, but he said it again and then leaned across to me, cutting through the loud music that seemed to be coming in through the open frontage from a bar across the street. "I'm just saying you look like a civilised chap," he said. "And the Cypriot shite is like drinking creamy fucking gasoline with the strength of pisswater. The Guinness is three times the price but at least its *real*." He was

34

already pouring it without me saying a word. "You know, it's cheaper to wash your car with Cypriot lager than it is using water. If you want your car even fucking dirtier than when you started out, that is." And he put the pint at my wrist. I didn't want it, but I paid for it.

"Do you know Furkan?" I said, baulking at the price of the drink.

"You mean Furkan Balaban? Yeah, sure. Everyone knows Furkan. You a friend of his?"

I felt as though I was heading down an avenue with no goal in sight. What was the attraction to this Furkan? I had seen something in him when he broke up that fight in the square, something I had only ever seen in the criminal fraternity back home. An authority that held something beyond the governance of law. I strongly suspected he would know the Russians on the island. Few people commanded the kind of presence I had seen from Furkan without being crooks.

"Do you know Illiarion Prostakov?"

"A Russian? There's a lot of them about, although not as many in Napa as rumour has it." He seemed to warm to his subject. "They tend to be in the north of the island, away from the barracks. Not that the soldiers would give a fuck about that sort of thing, but the Russians are..." he searched for a word, "... discreet."

"Discreet?"

"They don't see the need to get into trouble if it can be avoided. Why are you asking about Russians?"

I sipped my beer, and decided to follow my own version of discreetness. "A friend of mine is doing some work for him and I wanted to check he's legit," I said.

"Ha!" said the Irishman, and it was not a laugh but a blank straightforward exclamation. "He's not."

"So you do know him."

35

"Never fucking heard of him, mate, but I guarantee he's fucking Mafia if he's out here."

He was serving someone else now, and trying to keep his voice down through two yards of blasting music.

"I hear the Russians bring their own girls over with them," I said. "Seems an odd business decision when there are so many already out here."

The connection between us changed at that moment. He sighed and his shoulders broadened and he finished up serving his customer and sidled toward me.

"I get it," he said. "You're looking for someone. A relative? Maybe even your fucking daughter? Well, let me tell you something for no charge: I wish you all the luck in the world, but you need to shut the fuck up or get out of my pub."

He was close to me, leaning across my pint, close enough to see the reds of his eyes and smell the smoke on his breath, and his eyes were a strange mixture of soft and hard.

"You've got me wrong there," I said. "But consider the matter closed."

"Good," he said, and straightened up and the mood lifted. "I'll tell you one thing though, before we do move on and forget you ever asked: Furkan Balaban won't have any answers for you if it's girls you're looking for; I mean I've no doubt he can introduce you to some very nice ladies because he moves in those kind of circles, but he's not the guy you think he is if you're after him for all that shite."

I looked the barman up and down: his green tied shorts, his white T-shirt with faded Pogues album cover pulled taut over his beer belly – he was making clear that whatever circles Furkan mixed in they were not *his* circles. But an Irish barman in his fifties in Ayia Napa knows everyone twice.

"You staying in Napa?" he went on.

"Protaras," I said.

"At least you'll get some sleep," he laughed.

"I need to eat," I said and he pointed readily with a sausage of a forefinger to a bar across the street.

"Can't go wrong," he said. "Pork chops the size of dartboards."

The new bar was more ready for the party group, polystyrene rocks forming dimly-lit booths, of which I took one that looked out over the street whilst still concealing me as much as it could. For Napa, the night was young, and strolling around you could still see the odd tourist who would not be found here deeper into the night – older couples; an obviously younger German couple all blonde hair and innocent perspectives. I ate my pork chops – not quite the size of dartboards but they were large enough to give credence to the exaggeration – and wondered how long I would have to sit there before I saw the whole of what Napa had to offer. I ordered a beer, and then another, and remained at my spot in silence until the sun fell and the lights went up casting a stage-like heat across the street. Before too long things got louder – not the music, as that was consistently loud, neighbouring venues competing like opposing storm winds – but the street began to fill with groups of young people, all screeching, lolloping, all of them on the prowl. Groups of lads, groups of girls, each of them pecked at by the street staff paid to try and lure passing packs into one of the open-front bars that seemed to go on and on like market stalls. It was a circus from where I was sitting, and one that was peopled with a twisted idea of attractiveness, peopled with those both blessed with good looks and those not so much, all down in the same shallow waters of forced equality.

The odd scooter parped and swerved through on occasion, some of them with Cypriots riding, but mainly it was the predictable mess of sunburnt Western youngsters strutting their stuff with bare chests for the boys and gleaming strap marks along mauve shoulders for the girls. The one exception was odd indeed, and the sign that beneath Napa was a real town with miscreants and chancers grifting the underbelly. A small man wearing nothing – not even on his feet – but a pair of green denim cut-off shorts, and a green denim truckers cap pulled right down over his eyes, walked gingerly past the bar. He looked, even at some distance, like he was experiencing the street through a veil. His small naked torso was covered in ill-defined tattoos that went up his neck and presumably under his hat. He walked with a bit of a trot, there was something bird-like – no, lizard-like – about him. He looked cold, like a razor's edge. I watched him passing, half-expecting him to beg for coins in his cap from passers-by, or go through the bins of the bars and stores that piled up in the alleys, but he just went on, lightly bobbing on the balls of his feet. I knew even from this distance that there was something not right about him, something unkind about him.

I was thinking about Francis – he knew Napa; Prostakov had said he had found him here. Francis had not been a 'debauchee', as he liked to call them – as he had sometimes called *me*. He enjoyed drinking, and could do it long into the night if the accompanying conversation held him in sway. He had dabbled with drugs in the 'forties and 'fifties, so far as I knew, but he claimed to never have found a state that suited him aside from liquor. Something about the medium of the drug, he used to say; liquid has nobleness to it, unlike powder and weed, which if you rubbed it between your fingertips would smudge like charcoal. Chemicals were another thing altogether. In his day, popping pills was a Californian way to drop out. He had been over there in the 'forties, in Los Angeles, at the pool parties, declining the waiters who held out trays of barbiturates like they were *hors d ouvres*, avoiding the girls that he knew on sight were too young, too strung out. *That s* what chemicals did, he told me once; they make you do unclean things. He knew how to read people, how to watch them. Napa would have interested him.

I had been minding my own business for a few hours, slowly making my way through some light beers, thinking winding thoughts like this, when I became aware someone was standing over me.

"I'm Tara." The woman who was introducing herself was in her mid-fifties; she had cropped white hair that spiked like crystals above a beaming face of dense Mediterranean tan. As she smiled down at me in my seat, her face pulled into numerous leathery lines up her cheeks and across her forehead. It was a generous and welcoming sight, and I found myself smiling back up at her as a matter of reflex.

"Hello Tara," I said, half-raising my glass to her, not really sure what else to say.

"I just wanted to check you were okay," she said, her smile not dropping. It was not a fake smile, and it was not a ditsy one, it was the smile of a person broadly aware of her place in this immediate life; it was confident and at-home, and had the measure of every inch of the bar.

"There's not a problem, is there?" I said.

"Not at all. I work here. Or rather, I help out. My partner owns the place. Which means I suppose I have a certain vested interest when I'm on the premises. And I seem to have some sort of rank. So I was just seeing how everything was going and the waiter pointed you out and said you had been here a while on your own, and seeing as you looked British I thought I'd come over and say hello."

The smile I noticed now was as awkward as it was warm.

"Isn't everyone here British?" I said.

"True. But you seem more my type."

"Your type?"

"I'm on a mission, and I need an easy subject. I'm trying to put the effort in, you see. Into the business. The Ayia Napa nightlife is not my *usual* crowd."

"Okay," I said. "Next question: why did the waiter point me out?"

"I was asking."

"I see."

"My boyfriend and I had a fight. My partner. I mentioned him."

"Yes."

"I am trying to make up by showing a more active interest in his work, as he is so very helpful with mine."

"And what is your business?" I said.

"Well here's the test," Tara said.

"A test?"

"Of whether I was right in thinking you were more my type." She sat on the bench next to me in the booth. "I am an art dealer."

I let out a short bark of a laugh, half-expecting this to be some kind of put-on.

"That is one helluva coincidence," I said. "I am an artist."

She grabbed my forearm and swayed back and fore, her eyebrows curving and those lines erupting all over her face. "You are *fucking* with me."

"I am not." We were both sniggering.

"The waiter – Angelo, I think – he said *my type* didn't really come in here, because *my type* only come to Napa in the daytime and are home to bed by the time the vodka shots come out." She shouted *HA!* and waved her fingers toward Angelo like a firing pistol. "We don't get many artists in Napa and I spotted you a mile off."

She appeared to make herself comfortable at the table, took a cigarette out of a box of Sobranie Blacks and offered me one.

"So what brings you here, a dealer with no-one to deal?" I said.

"Oh, love brings me here. I came here for love. Love love love. And now I have my own gallery. Just up on the top road. The classy stretch of Napa." She winked. "It's just my base. But I do business all around – Athens, Sofia, Rome, Tel Aviv. Ha! It always sounds so stupid saying that in here."

"You have a gallery?" I said. "You knew Francis Benthem?"

40

Her smile dropped but not mirthlessly. It was in recognition of the continuing coincidences.

"You know Francis," she said. "You are in Cyprus for him – this is making sense now. How is he?"

I was surprised.

"Francis passed away," I said. "I came for his funeral."

"Oh no," Tara said and put her hand to her mouth.

"You weren't invited to the funeral?"

"It's been a few years, I have to admit. And I don't really know who would have thought to invite me."

"He was working for a man named Illarion Prostakov. Do you know him?" Tara shook her head and leaned back on the bench. "Sorry to be the bearer of bad news," I said.

"That was quite a five minutes meeting you," she said, and smiled rather sadly at me. "Furkan will be sad; he liked Francis a great deal." And she waved wildly past me at the figure coming into the bar through the open front. It was Furkan Balaban.

"You know Furkan?" I said, as much in admission of fate as anything.

"This is his place," Tara said, having caught his attention. "Furkan, my darling love, I found this lost soul."

Furkan looked me up and down and held out his hand – he was much less intimidating than I had taken him for the previous day. In fact, he had a rather placid demeanour, albeit bolstered by his muscular build.

"You've been asking after me," he said. We shook hands. "You were at the bar yesterday when that fight broke out."

"Both," I said.

"You didn't tell me you'd been looking for Furkan," Tara said and slapped me playfully across the shoulder.

"I didn't know you knew each other."

"Have a drink with us," Furkan said and gestured to Angelo at the bar. Angelo very quickly came over with a beer, a gin and tonic and a short strong coffee for Furkan, the aroma of which overpowered anything else within ten yards of our table. Furkan sat next to Tara in the booth and raised his coffee in salutation and knocked it back in one with a jerk of the head.

"Francis Benthem passed away," Tara said.

Furkan nodded slightly. "That is sad news. I liked Francis. He was in Napa?"

"We buried him yesterday," I said.

"Of course. There was a service in Paralimni. That is why you were at my bar there."

"Forgive me for being forward, Furkan," I said, "but you struck me yesterday as the kind of person who knows everything that goes on on an island like this."

I was beginning to feel the beer and the humidity take hold of me. Instead of answering, Furkan looked at Tara.

"Furkan is looked up to," she said, tapping her boyfriend affectionately on his cheek with the palm of her hand. "What is it you wanted to know?"

And I really couldn't put my finger on it. Perhaps it was the beer, mixed with the climate, but I wasn't thinking straight. I wasn't sure if I had ever known what it was I wanted to ask Furkan. He seemed a man to ally with. And he was *of* the place, not an insurgent. I wanted to know more about Cyprus, more about the place Francis had spent his final years. Something deep down was nagging at me, something about Francis's nature that kept bringing me back to the fact all of this was so out of sync with the man I had known and admired. The man who had influenced me more than any other living being.

"Didn't you think Cyprus was a strange place for Francis Benthem to end up?" It was the closest I could come to a sentence that reflected in some way my thoughts.

Furkan shrugged. "He always just seemed to be Francis to me," he said.

"Francis was a man looking for a window," Tara said. "His previous being didn't really seem to come into it."

It was an answer good enough to put an end to the avenue of thought, and it was meant to do just that. For punctuation, Tara and Furkan kissed with a smile – she was at least fifteen years his senior, but there was a power between them that drew those years closer together.

"I thought you two were fighting," I said.

They both laughed.

"That was yesterday," Furkan said. He stood. "It's really nice to meet you," he said to me and shook my hand again. "You'll stick around?"

"Sure," I replied. I said to Tara when he had gone, "He is a very likeable chap."

"He changed everything for me," she said wistfully. "I've been lucky, of course. I was living in London, very successful. I found the art world easy. The whole business. But I was unhappy – unhappily married. I met Furkan one night and that was that. I was able to come here and keep my business going in part. You'll find Cyprus is full of Brits with stories like that."

"I didn't know," I said.

"Other people's lives are always like a secret when you're in London," Tara said. "You are over from London?"

"Near enough," I said.

"You have a wife or equivalent?"

"A girlfriend."

"But she's not here with you – kids or falling out?"

"We don't have kids."

Tara clinked my beer with her gin and tonic tumbler. "Well, there's just as many closed doors here when you get to know the place as anywhere else."

"Closed doors?"

"It's an island of runaways," Tara said. "Brits, Russians, Greeks."

"How are the Greeks runaways?"

"From the north. You know the history of the island?"

"Not in any detail," I said.

"Especially around here. Second generation Greeks driven from their homes when the Turkish invaded in 'seventy-four. It's all still bubbling under the surface. And you know about the partition?"

"There is a wall?"

"Right across the island. The Turks have the north and the Greeks have the south. It's largely a fence, of course, but try cutting through it and they'll fucking shoot you dead."

"That's serious."

"It's an island for those who cannot settle. Those who have no intention of settling."

"You seem pretty settled," I said.

"Well, I am many things – *happy*, for one – but I don't think of myself as settled. I love this island. I love Napa. I love my work and I love Furkan. But who knows? I'm old enough to know life doesn't care about any individual enough to put misery on hold out of politeness. It could all open up at any moment and show the shit we are all made of."

The conversation had taken a turn, and Tara's infectious smile and energy suddenly seemed a long way off. So there was conflict within Tara just as there was conflict within all of us, and around all of us. It was becoming apparent that what I was doing was trying to weigh up the potential dangers of taking Prostakov up on his wild offer. But I needed to know if Prostakov had a name, and if people like Furkan knew of it. Reputation is everything in these enclaves, and it was no different here I would guess than in the Soho I had known, for both artists and the flies that buzzed around the artists. The relationships moved around the enclave, arteries connecting one interest, one ambition, to another, streets away. I knew if Prostakov was into some shit, then Furkan would know who he was.

"This place *will* surprise you," Tara said, as if reading my mind.

I thought for a moment. "I think I am about to do something stupid."

"In Cyprus you only need ask yourself one question," Tara said, deadly serious. "Is it out of desperation?"

"The guy that Francis ended up working for, the Russian, I am unsure how to read him. But part of me is sure Francis would never have gotten himself involved with anyone of dubious morality. I mean, I think he might have girls on his property – they could very well be prostitutes – like he is running sex workers from his house. And then part of me thinks they could be his nieces and I am being a godawful fucking racist for thinking every Russian with a couple of young girls by his pool is a Mafia pimp."

Tara laughed at this, and rolled her eyes.

"This is Cyprus," she said. "You won't be far off the mark."

"And Furkan?"

Her expression became cooler.

"Yesterday I saw him break up a street fight without throwing so much as a naughty word around the place. That is some clout."

"You're wrong about Furkan if you think he's a crook," she said.

"I don't mean anything by it," I said. "I guess I'm just looking for someone to do one of two things."

"And they are?"

"Either tell me to go home or ram my head into a wall."

"Both of which stop you from taking the Russian up on his offer."

"I have had a handful of conversations in the last twenty-four hours, and they are not making anything clearer."

"Again: welcome to Cyprus." Tara drained her glass. "Don't feel bad you don't understand it your first day. All those people out there, they come to get fucked up. They'll go back to Britain and sit under their florescent lights in their grey offices and their entire lives will revolve around just how fucked up they manage to get every year for a week in Ayia Napa. But that's not why *you're* here. That's not why *I'm* here. It's like us and them are separated by a six-inch pane of glass. We live in the real world with shades of colour and depths of darkness, and they live in the grey, and then BOOM a week of bright light and loud music. You look like I'm pulling the colour right out of your cheeks. What I'm saying is, you will never find another place like this. And you might not like it, but you won't be able to shake free. Because it is like a fantasy realm. All different creatures. All different kingdoms. Crammed onto this little rock."

"So you think I should stay, is that what you're saying?" I purposely broke the philosophising and we both laughed.

"I'm saying you should stay, of course I am," Tara said and slapped my shoulder.

She called over to Angelo for another round of drinks.

"It has been quite a sight," I said. "I was enjoying people-watching before you came over."

"It could be reasonably argued that people-watching is better than people-interacting."

"Sounds like something Francis would have said."

The drinks arrived.

"And stay the fuck away from that guy." Tara pointed out to the street where I could see the small tattooed man coming back into frame from the direction he had earlier walked. He was such a strange creature, and he moved almost as if in a lazy dance, deep into the night, his hands out in front of him as if he was waltzing alone. It was difficult to make out his face, such was the light and the tattoos, which I could now see were across his face as well as up his neck.

"I noticed him earlier," I said.

"That's Stelly," Tara said.

"Who is he?"

She puffed out her cheeks.

"That's some question. For another night. Just stay out of his way. Never take any pill he ever offers you. Never find yourself alone with him. Just stay out of his way."

"You think there's a danger?"

Tara curved her neck and groaned.

"You've been looking for advice all night," she said. "So fucking take some."

Five

I stopped drinking early that night, taking a taxi back to Protaras for supper, rather than soldiering on into the forgotten tips of a heavy session, which was my more common strategy. I stayed up late into the night regardless, perched up on my balcony allowing my thoughts to drift through the mesh of the starlit sky. I had called Clare and this had left me feeling positive. I had told her of an offer, of a commission.

"I suppose congratulations are in order," she said. Clare was never spiteful, never bitter, but at her most caustic she came across as defeated, disappointed, and that is what she sounded like here. "So you'll be out there a little while longer, and then home with the money? I can ask dad for a short term loan until you get back."

"I think we can leave your father out of this," I said.

"Nice to hear you have your zing back," she said. "I find it difficult when you're all contrite, like the last time we spoke."

She kept saying she couldn't speak for long as she was at her niece's birthday party and family members kept poking their heads in to ask where she was. It sounded busy behind her.

"I'm going up to talk to the gentleman who commissioned me today and I'm going to see about getting some money up front," I said, unsure of any of this.

"My dad's here now," Clare said. "And he's in a good mood, so I'm going to ask him today. You have to remember I am here, living in that place now, with all this hanging over me. You just left."

"And now I have the means to sort everything out."

"And I'm happy about that, I really am. But if it doesn't come off…"

Her voice trailed, spun off into the stars.

I said to Illie the next day that my decision to take him up on his offer was based on how clear I had found the night sky. "I cannot bring myself to go back to the dank roof of England quite yet. I think it's good for the mind and we'll see what it does to my painting."

Illie laughed and shook me by the hand. "I will be honest with you; I am not too concerned as to your reasons for saying yes, but I am glad you see a future here."

"We do need to clear up a few things before I sign anything," I said.

"There will be no signing."

"Just a figure of speech." Although I hadn't meant it as such.

Illie was excitable, prowling almost.

"I need some of the payment up front," I said. I had not wanted to go into details as to why, but he said nothing to my demand, just bobbed his head and continued to pace, a smile coming to and then going from his face. I went on, wary of the silence. "I have some matters I need to clear up first if I am to stay with you for a while." Silence. "Just need to set some things in order."

"You owe money," he said finally. "I understand. I do not approve of getting into such ways, but we have to admit to ourselves it is the way of the world. Debt. It will eat you up. As if the world wasn't dangerous enough, we do this to ourselves." And he left the room and came back a few moments later with an envelope and handed it to me. I peeled back the opening and saw the cash. It was a huge amount, in sterling, too much to count. Reflexively, I shut the envelope quickly, as if someone might be watching.

"So we'll send for your things from the hotel. Write down your details here and I'll send Viktor." He pushed a pad and pencil across the kitchen top toward me, and, still a little dazed from the envelope of cash, I wrote down the hotel and room number. As I stood over the notepad, the envelope of money in my hand like a cold wet fish, I thought about what Clare would say if I had given her details of this proposition. She knew very well my ability to embalm myself in morally complicated environments. She would not have been all that surprised at this, and she was no doubt concocting her own version of events back home, feet up on the sofa, wine glass in hand, giving me a heinous narrative.

"We need to talk about the work," I said, snapping myself out of it. "I need to know what it is you require me to do."

"Paint," he said.

"Yes, you said that. But what?"

Illie looked mischievous. He had stopped pacing, and now looked at me, leaning on his fists on the kitchen top. He invited me to continue.

"I know this one guy," I said. "He had a nice number in one of the southern states in the United States. A university commissioned him to paint a series of former slave plantations across the county. He had a few years' work out of it and, well, it changed his life in many ways…"

Illie cut me off. "Is this what you think you're here for?"

"I have been going over in my mind what I might be here for," I said.

Illie nodded, his fists still planted onto the kitchen top. "Well, yesterday I did not know I could trust you."

"And today is different?"

"Today you have agreed to come and live here."

Perhaps surprisingly, this was the first time I had felt an inclination to have concern for my liberty. It had not occurred to me this might be, in Illie's eyes at least, a lifetime appointment. I

50

was quite clearly a different proposition to Francis. I was half his age for a start, and nothing about me would speak of a man looking for somewhere to see out his earthly years in quiet. I suddenly felt as though I knew nothing, and that the money, the promise of the expunging of all my problems, had blinded me to greater problems.

"I cannot stay here indefinitely, Illie," I said.

"The other people on the property are simply friends of mine visiting for a holiday," Illie said.

"Why didn't you tell me that yesterday?"

"Because it was none of your business yesterday," he said. "You met them at the funeral, anyway. I do not see what is so important."

"Are they going to be related to my work?"

Illie's shoulders unknotted and he gazed out of the window across the way to the woodland. "I have been thinking of you as a new friend. But all these questions. Francis never had so many questions."

"I just need to know."

"And yet I don't get the feeling that you are thinking of pulling out." And he looked at the wad of cash I still held in my hand.

He had me, in actual fact. I was there for the money now, no backing out. But I needed him to know I would not be part of whatever it was he had going on up here.

"I am not Francis," I said defiantly.

"It took Francis months before he could understand what it was I required of him. He stayed here, spent much of his time on the balcony of that tower, overlooking the wood I planted in the valley, drinking his expensive brandy. Sometimes *my* expensive brandy. And then sometimes we drank on that balcony together. We talked. We explored ideas. He helped me on my journey, and then he painted what I needed. He did it meticulously and without complaint."

51

Francis once said to me that when he was lecturing he could split a lecture hall between those artists who would sip up the bullshit and those who needed more than that – the students who needed more were always in the minority, he said, sometimes painfully small in number, but these were the ones he trusted to create great work, to go places. I had been one of those students.

Illie smacked his lips and dipped his head. He was thinking his way out of a growing frustration with me.

"I do not need you to paint landscapes for me, not like that plantation painter you talked about," he said.

"Family portraits?" I smiled as I asked.

Illie ran his hand across his jaw, before saying in a low voice, "I came here ten years ago, you know? People thought I was leaving too much behind, but the truth is, my wife had died, and we had never had children together, so I felt I was leaving nothing at all behind. Businesses? Ah, these are just things to keep our hands occupied. They do not mean anything. It is only love that means things in life, you know? I learned of that late in life, I suppose. So I came here. The scene of some good times in my youth. I had always known that I would come back. I had hoped I would come to live here with my wife, but that was not to be."

"I'm sorry about your wife," I said.

"You think at first when she dies that everything is over. But it is not. Things go on and eventually the clouds thin out and you have to figure out what it is you are going to fill the days with. Well, in those dark days I had seen much. I had looked over our time together, and then gone further. It was like living a life in reverse. And I saw a central truth to myself, you know? Very few of us live the last years the same person that we were for those first years."

He was making less sense to me the further his speech went on, and as he went even further he began to mix Russian phrases, and then entire Russian sentences, and he was no longer really addressing me at all, but was talking to the air between us.

Eventually I held on to his wrist, not forcefully, but with something close to affection, and I said, "Illie, I want to know how I can help, like Francis helped."

He looked me in the eyes, and his were only partially focussed, partially glassy, and a little bloodshot, and he said, "I need you to paint. I need this. Francis kept me sane much of the time." He laughed, and it was light, not at all desperate or reaching. "We would sit on that balcony and talk and drink and then I would come back here to the house and sleep it all off and in the morning I would come back to the tower and he would have that day's painting for me, and he would often be asleep in the chair or up in the bed by the time I came back, so I would tiptoe around and pick up the painting and take it with me and leave him sleeping. And the next night we would do the same again, and then again, and he would paint and I would take it, and the circle went on."

"But what did he paint for you, Illie?"

He looked at me fully, the glassiness dissipating in his eyes.

"I want you to paint my dreams," he said.

Six

Taking the money of a madman was not my primary concern those first few days; no, it was rather that I had no holding, no firm footing for delivering anything on expectation. I held that envelope of cash for much of the night. I did not take a single note out, didn't sniff it, roll around in it. I just held it. Viktor took me to the Western Union in Napa, a room of heavy odours and deep auburn paint peeling off the walls. I would not have felt safe with that amount of cash in there had Viktor not stood at my arm. At one point he smiled broadly and nudged me on the shoulder as the teller licked his thumb and counted out the cash onto the worktop, and he said to me, "You paint Mr Prostakov's dreams, and there is your dream right there, in the dirty hands of a stranger." He found this very amusing, even to the point where I cracked a smile too.

Illie had requested nothing from me apart from my relaxation for as long as I needed. Viktor was instructed to be my right arm – an offer I waved away. I suspected Francis might have lapped this up when it was offered to him. There was a theory on this kind of madness that Francis had talked about that I was struggling to bring to mind. The madness of the wealthy is a special kind of delusion, he said. It was more often than not about making a mark, and the madness stemmed from either failure or the cowardice of disappointment at failure. Francis had spent a short time in a sanatorium just before his return from Hollywood after the war, and much of his work around that time was awash with what critics thought was the Californian sunshine, but I always thought it was the anaesthetised white of the ward he had been interned on.

It was not the same light here, anyway. Francis had given up on flooding with light long before I knew him, and this burnished landscape fitted in with his philosophy very well indeed. Light wrestled with dark, and was always just an inch from tapping out for good. Darkness was where it was at for Francis. There was no such thing as pitch light, after all.

Francis had said there is a reason we believe we are hurtling toward the light, and that is because none of us could ever really imagine it. Light and death were the great mysteries, and he had no time – we, as men, had no time – to try and solve mysteries like that. He would rumble around in the shadows. He was not a god.

I understood him better now than I ever did when he lectured me. Sometimes, for me, back when he was my mentor, spit and fire was all I needed to get me to the canvas. And now? Illie had not needed to sermonise. I had gone for the money – now there's a shadow for you. Of course, it was not the cash I found attractive – I can be honest about that. I needed Clare to think better of me. That was what the money bought me. She could up and leave, so long as she did not think poorly of me as she went. I knew, even at my lowest points, that people can be kind to one another, and I had all my life cared as much for the kind thoughts of good people as I disregarded the sentiments of everybody else. Francis had seen this in me, had called it my curse, and curled his lip into a rakish smile as he raised a glass and said so.

That's not to say I was blind to the madman. Paint his dreams. I repeated the line several times as I walked the dusty grounds of the house, watched the sun dip over the hills beyond the flatlands of the south east. I had left Illie in the main house. He had advised me to go and relax, take in some of the evening warmth and prepare for dinner. "I have left a welcome gift for you in the tower," he said, and he had. A bottle of Hennessy Paradis Cognac waited for me on the table that Francis had used for his tobacco and pipe. I poured a gutsy quadruple measure into a tumbler, almost in defiance of the craft and expense of the plonk, and walked out into the amber light.

Paint my dreams.

The more I went over the phrase in my head, the more I could understand it in relation to the peculiar isolation of this place, and the peculiar dryness of Cyprus. There seemed to be nothing solid about the place, nothing that could offer up a real definition. The Mediterranean was surrounded by nations who had powerful ideas of what they were, and those nations were peopled with folk who had no problem signing up to and defending those definitions. Politics could cause problems – all the countries had had bloody eras at some point – but they were internal struggles, like a hand fighting for superiority inside a glove. But Cyprus had nothing like that about it. I had been there just a few days and it seemed an island of shipwrecked souls. Even the tourists seemed to not know or care where they had landed. Illie seemed an anomaly, even in my limited experience. He had hinted at having returned to a place he had fond memories of. That was not so unusual in people closer to the end of their lives than the beginning. He had wavered as he mentioned his wife, and it was easy to see that a man who had achieved a great deal, perhaps against great odds, came home every night to something safe, constant, salvational. It's difficult to really understand how to go on in the absence of such a presence. I thought of Clare and how benign would be her inevitable departure from my life. My only thought was making sure that when she left she could tell people that I did not leave her financially screwed. A low bar.

I took a swig of the brandy. It had a remarkable body to it and I could feel the blood awaken from my cheeks to my forehead. I would have sworn in court that the liquid went down through me and lit me up every inch as it went like an x-ray machine. I was probably revelling a little in the feeling when I heard the tentative sound of footsteps in gravel, made all the more succinct by my heightened state. And so I startled a bit – my eyes had been closed as I enjoyed the brandy, and opening them I stumbled a little. I must have looked quite drunk.

In the hazy light was a young girl, and it took me a few blinks before I recognised her as one of the girls from the funeral.

"Illie says dinner is ready," she said. And when I didn't speak, just glared at her, she said, "He sent me for you."

"Yes, of course, of course," I said, not sure why I was coming across as so dishevelled. "Thanks for fetching me."

I followed her back toward the house, and we went on without speaking, she a few yards ahead of me, placing her dainty steps along the path in the lowering light. She was not leading me back to the house, however, and as we turned to head down to the pool we were also met with the billowing smell of barbecue. Down past the pool was a patio area, obscured from the path by poplar trees, and there on garden furniture was the other girl and the man.

"Our new company," the man said without getting up. Also in this secluded den was a bar made out of timber, complete with refrigeration units and thatched roof. The girl who had fetched me went to it and asked what I would like to drink. I looked around – no Illie to be seen – and I felt that Hennessy sending shoots through my blood stream. I then noticed I still had the empty brandy glass in my hand. I put it on the table and politely asked for a coke.

As I took a seat the man introduced himself as Evgeny. "And these are my daughters, Dina and Darya. Hard to believe, I know, that I could have been responsible for such beauties." He said this with a personable smile from behind aviators and a puff of smoke, but the smile was stale, it hung on his jaw like an ignored painting in a stately home. He was a markedly handsome man, with that cool demeanour Francis used to call 'Vintage Vegas'. Next to their father, Dina and Darya looked like children, whereas away from his presence they came across as young women. That Russian bone structure meant they would probably look twenty-one until their mid-forties. Darya was the older, the one who had fetched me, with the slightly broader face and the eyes that had a somewhat more affirming glare to them. Dina was a few years younger – fourteen I was to find out later, and Darya was sixteen – and she was quieter for it, her eyes were often cast away to nothing or down to the ground. But for that she seemed happy, not dissimilar to any other fourteen-year-old girl. We talked idly for a while, Evgeny asking about me and then my work when I said I was an artist. It was Dina who was attending to the barbecue, a skill Evgeny proudly noted was amongst the many of his daughters'. "I have never really been one for cooking," he said and laughed. "They get everything from books, you know? Which I find encouragingly old-fashioned."

"They have been home-schooled?" I said.

"Home is the only school worth a spit," Evgeny said. "Did you learn to paint doing sums on a wet afternoon?"

I thought about explaining how mathematics had played an important part of my early development, but Evgeny was enjoying his audience, and I was allowing him to draw that energy from my poised silence.

"England is a lot like Russia," he went on. "You really have to pull away to make a mark. Otherwise it's all mapped out for you, no? You're born, you serve, you die."

"I didn't pay enough attention at school," I said. There was a pause. "Much to the anger of my parents."

Evgeny looked at me side-on with a straight mouth, my reflection in his aviators bulbous, like peering into the back of a spoon.

Steaks were the order of the evening, and as they were served up with potato salad and grilled Halloumi, Evgeny pointed out just how difficult it was to get beef on the island. "Illie likes to impress us with his exotic tastes," he said. "Exotic for Cyprus."

"Are you staying long?" I said at one point, tucking into the food, which Dina had cooked to perfection.

The question seemed to change the mood a little, and all three of them looked at me and then each other and it seemed as though they each might have had different answers.

"It's not really like that," Evgeny said.

"Illie said you were visiting from Russia on holiday," I said.

"We are here indefinitely," said Darya.

"Eat your food," Evgeny said to her.

"You do excellent food," I said to Dina to break a perceptibly awkward moment. "Your father doesn't mind you making American dishes?" I laughed as I said it, but my company showed no response.

For a while then we all ate in silence, the sun now down. I asked why Illie had not joined us, and Evgeny said Illie dined alone in the evening always. "I see him walking sometimes," Darya said.

I felt as if nobody knew the whole picture, and if you pulled us all together into one space there was a chance – but not a certainty – you could build a real narrative with a beginning, middle and end. But as it was, I just ate my food, and let the scraps of conversation fall where they might.

What the story of Darya and Dina was, I could only guess. They didn't look like I would have imagined entrapped girls to look. If I understood anything of the sex trade it was that behind the scenes it all came down to one thing: ownership. And these girls didn't seem like anyone's property. That Dina and Darya were sisters was undeniable, and there was a fair chance Evgeny was their father – although they bore no real genetic resemblance, they did have a warmth between them, the three of them. Dina leaned on the arm of Evgeny's chair and said, "May I now, papa?" and he looked at his watch, and she said, "It has been thirty minutes, I counted it down myself," and Evgeny thought for a moment and then said, "Okay," and Dina quickly pulled her blouse up off over her head to reveal her bikini and ran to dive into the pool.

"I teach her not to swim for at least thirty minutes after a meal," he said when he noticed my inquisitive face. "She loves to swim."

Those few hours with Evgeny Pajari and his two daughters, I forgot I was on an island populated by human versions of mismatched furniture. The conversation settled, we all relaxed, I drank a little wine – not too much – and Evgeny asked me questions about art, most of which I could not answer. We parted with a pat to the back, and a kiss on each cheek from both girls, and I waved as I made my way along the ridge to the tower in the burnt brown of the darkness. I awoke the next morning in Francis's bed on the mezzanine of the tower, the beneficiary of the soundest sleep of my adult life.

Seven

The day had drifted away from me, as I imagined a number of them would from now on; me in my tower, my patron in his castle, a fabricated wood between us. I walked to the pool in what must have been the afternoon. I did not see another soul. There had been a hamper left for me in the studio space of the tower – ham, cheeses, bread and a selection of juices – and so I picked at that. I slept ten hours through the night and then still napped twice the following day, for twenty minutes at around noon, and then for twenty more after my lunch. This was the pattern of that following week. The heat was delightful, not at all oppressive or discomforting, and it came across the plains and up from the shallow tresses of the valley with a thin breeze in tow. Time was no thing. The air seemed clean. I might have been the last man on earth if indeed this little spot reminded me of Earth all that much.

And then as the sun hung over in the sky, I saw from my recliner on the balcony a figure coming along the ridge between the wood and the pool; broad, with shoulders leading – Viktor. He had come to invite me – *instruct* me would be more accurate, as the invitation was a polite formality – to dine out that evening with Illie. I didn't welcome the notion, I must admit. It had been a long time since the world had been this quiet for me, and I was in no immediate rush to let the peacefulness slip away.

And it could not have slipped away more abruptly than it did.

Illie was dressed in that heavy-smart way older men of money manage to carry off. He was perfectly tanned and groomed, his tailored white shirt with double cuffs was open two buttons down from his neck allowing short wisps of white hair to peek out from his acorn-coloured chest. The shirt defined his impressive athletic physique (for his age) and brought him down in a triangle to his waist, where a golden buckle separated his shirt from his slacks. He wore no socks with glistening black espadrilles. Although he was dressed with a hustler's sense of taste, he did look younger, and it occurred to me here that I wouldn't have known exactly the age to put him at. Sixty? But the day before, in the kitchen, he could have been eighty-five, (albeit an eighty-five capable of kicking my arse).

I myself on the other hand was tidy and clean, but that was about as far as it went. Illie looked me up and down as we headed for the car in the driveway and he said, "Ah, you'll do, but we'll have to kit you out now you're staying." And he slapped me on the shoulder.

We drove the short dusty journey down to Napa, with Viktor his imperious self in the driver's seat. I asked where we were going, but Illie just repeated that it didn't really matter and Napa was much like anywhere else, whilst being not quite like anywhere else. I waited for him to expand on the theory but Illie just grinned and looked out the window. Music played through the car speakers – I think it was Sibelius, although I have never been good at identifying any music written before nineteen sixty-three.

Viktor pulled up on the main drag in Napa, just as the streets were beginning to get busy.

"You had heard of this place before you came here?" Illie said before opening the door.

"Ayia Napa has a bit of reputation, yes," I said.

"Well, you may wonder tonight what attracts me to this place. If you can't figure it out by the time we leave then ask and I will tell you," he said.

62

As we entered a bar through an open front, I noticed Furkan's place just down the way and I began to get my bearings. Napa looked different from every vantage point, as if it was planned out by an amateur who couldn't tell a right angle from a kebab skewer. Some of it was a lack of familiarity with my surroundings, but something felt deeper, longer than that; it was like a fairground ride where the ground is made of boards that swing underfoot.

Inside the bar it was a breathless submerging into edgeless blacks, thick dark purples, and the diamond sparkles of chrome and glass. It made me feel slightly nauseous at first, and then anxious, as if I was slipping into an amniotic sack. And for all I knew everybody else in there felt the same way, as it was impossible to make out any more than thirty per cent of a face at any one time. The whole room was a merciless battle against the subtlety of shadow.

Illie was greeted warmly – as was I, as his guest – by almost everyone we passed, after the hefty gentlemen on the door. The owner, who was another Russian or thereabouts, came over and showed us to our table, and he and Illie talked quickly in Russian for the thirty-or-so steps it took us to reach it. Whether he was ordering for us I did not know, but beer and food soon arrived without any look at menus or a discussion about allergies or anything like that.

"It does not take long to get to know people here," Illie said, leaning across to me in our half-moon booth. The music in the place was a low ambient dance vibe, the sort of drawn-out bass lines that get under your skin rather than come down on top of you. Illie pointed out at one point that he liked this music – I guessed he liked this more than the Sibelius he had been playing in the Bentley – he said the music was like paint, and it filled all the cracks but didn't hide any protruding features. So conversation, to Illie, was a protruding feature. And by that measurement, it could be as ugly or as attractive as a human face.

"Did you bring Francis here?" I said. This was the first burning question of the evening. I could not, with all the power of my imagination, place Francis Benthem in this blackness.

Illie laughed, his head rocked back, and he nodded at me vigorously without saying a word, his eyes lighted with mischief and maybe more than a few stories of his nights out with Francis. "But not as much as where we're headed," he said.

Illie necked his drink with one sharp movement and without any ceremony, and so I followed suit and we left.

The Castle was on the next street over. A vast, intimidating, post-apocalyptic nightclub that went up two storeys and then down into the ground three or four more. It was loosely themed along medieval lines, but it took no more than a glance to see few historians of the period had been consulted on the set-up. Staff in peculiar garb of chainmail and Romano-Greco leathering showed off their oiled and perfect bodies near doorways, behind bars, and waiting tables. The entire establishment pulsed with the unintelligible music that throbbed and groaned around us – each floor had its own focus but they all had dance floors and DJs overseeing the dance floors like demigods, although a man revving a chainsaw into a microphone might have had the same sonic effect. As far as I could tell the deeper one went, the more the ground shook with sound, and the more the sound began to have an unsettling effect on the soul. The upper floors ran on air, and there were even pockets in which some people seemed to be in conversation. The top two floors were open to the elements, the very top floor simply being a gallery to look down upon the Roman forum of the floor below. It was the oblivious human shipwreck compared to the mouth of Hades that went on deep in the belly, several floors down. Everything was dark, and only occasionally a smile from a passer-by brought some blacklight teeth out, or a strobe hitting some fake bedrock walling. The atmosphere of the place was of confidence and the clientele, what could be seen of them, were ships passing in the night. This was the centre point of Napa, and it seemed to speak of a heavy silent truth to the place. So many people were just watching, gliding from one shadow to the next, drinking in the gloopy oceans before them. Beneath the heart-pounding of the music was a silence of people as dense as a black hole. It made telekinetic overtures that came out like heat waves and sizzled across the sparse beams of light. These silences torpedoed out of sight, and there is nothing more accurate than silence.

Illie of course knew the people we needed to know to get in, and to secure a civilised corner with table service on the mezzanine above the Roman forum. Again his man on the door spoke in the knotted codes of the Russian tongue, and even though Illie seemed to assure him I was sound, he still spoke hushed and bent to Illie's ear.

"I used to think this was not for me," Illie said when we were sitting. "But when my wife died I decided it was important to keep in touch with the world."

"*This* is the world?" I said. I ordered a scotch and coke but had no idea what came, perhaps some Cypriot version of scotch.

"I am an old man, although I don't like to admit it," Illie said. "I am not so special in that regard."

I figured he came here because it didn't matter – this was not a nightclub with any reference points. There seemed to be no cliques, no trends, no movements.

I wanted to ask Illie about the brief-of-sorts he had given me – I wanted to know what he meant by having me paint his dreams. I wanted to believe he was not a senile old man, trying to find some meaning in this strange existence he had carved out for himself in the aftermath of his wife's death. But it never felt right to do so. Something about Napa, something about being around Illie, made it feel as if things would come about in their own time.

"You said Francis liked this place," I said.

"Oh, yes. You see this is an exclusive club. The most exclusive in Napa. One thing gets you in here: notoriety. You think that would appeal to the Francis Benthem you knew?"

I said to Illie after a while that I was going to go explore, and he smiled generously and waved me away.

Never really one to go in for self-analysis, in the darkness and satanic pulsing of the tunnels and caves of The Castle, I nevertheless thought of something Clare had said to me when we had first started going out. It was a cliché that we had met at my own exhibition, and she had not known I was the artist she had come to see, and that I had spotted her the moment she entered the gallery – it was a good opening, although fewer in attendance than would have marked it out as a grand victory for my new collection. I stood next to her as she admired one of my cloudy, clumpy landscapes. The things said about me by critics at that time, in print and to my face, were always in terms of aggression; that my work was aggressive, angry, as if I imagined love was found in the carnage of a battlefield, as if love was a bouncing bomb, a cannonball, a swinging axe. But Clare spoke in that considered way of hers and she said that she felt the artist was in love with light. And in love with the silence that comes after the crash and bang. She thought that *I* was in love with light and silence. And of course that made me fall in love with *her*. And seeing me feel my way around the revolting rusty darkness of The Castle would have made her laugh.

I was thinking of this near a lower level bar, ordering a drink, when I became aware of something near my elbow. I looked up with a start, and saw a figure up close that at first was difficult to define. I thought first it was a naked child, but then I realised it was not a child, and although only wearing a pair of denim cut-off shorts, was hardly naked either – he was smeared in bad tattoos all across his taut tanned torso and up his arms and neck. It took a few moments but I did recognise him as the wretched

66

looking creature I had seen in the street from Furkan's bar. He had the cap pulled down low over his brow, and I noticed then too that he had no shoes. How had he gotten in here? Tara had given me his name, and I remembered it.

"Stelly," I said.

He looked me up and down like a reptile. His eyes were slits and his lips were crisp and pencil-thin. When he spoke, he felt the air with his tongue before every sentence.

"We know each other?" he said in broken English. His accent was swamp-thick.

"We have mutual friends," I said.

He was bobbing on his toes, this little lizard, his eyes barely open.

"Everybody know Stelly," he said.

"Is that right?"

He banged the palm of his hand on the bar and smiled at me with an indescribably ugly smile. His face clipped back in folds and his eyes turned black. I looked at the bar and then back at him. "A drink?" I said. And he bobbed a bit more and slapped his hand again on the top of the bar. "What you drinking?"

He smiled again and just pointed at mine. I ordered him the same. He picked it up and drank it in one, tonguing at the ice when the liquid was gone, and then he held the empty glass as if it was a trophy.

"That is good," he said, and smiled that awful smile again. "I no seen you around here before," he said.

"I'm new," I said.

"New in Kipros? You vacation?"

"Business," I said, somehow adopting his broken English.

"Where you from? You Ruski?" Stelly maintained his thin grin, and spoke in a darkly mocking tone. It was surely obvious I was not a Russian.

"No," I said. "British."

He bobbed up and down, looked around the room. The music heaved and pumped.

"I am doing some work for a Russian," I said. I'm not sure why – I think silence between us was even more unpalatable than talking to him.

"You work for Ruski?" His eyes came back to me. And with that Stelly put one of his stumpy little hands into the tight pockets of his shorts and handed me a small white pill. And then he looked me in the eye and the music seemed to quieten and my heartbeat seemed to slow.

"You have this," he said. "And I will find you later."

And he bobbed off, almost as if he was invisible to everyone but me. If his stench had not been so ugly and cruel I may have worried about the sexual edge to his final gift – it had certainly felt like a threat that was intended to hit me in a dark recess of some sexual playground he had assumed I frequented.

I was frozen to the spot for a few moments, thinking about the gateway to Hell that Stelly had just climbed out of and disappeared back into, and forgetting I had a pill in my hand. On remembering that last fact I spent a little while examining it, glaring at its small insignia of what seemed to be a crown or a fan or something. I don't know how long I had been doing it before I had a tap on the elbow.

"You're supposed to be a bit more discreet about that in here," the woman said. I jumped and dropped the bloody thing. She laughed. "Sorry," she said, and she bent over to pick it up for me.

"Oh god, no, it's not mine. Some fucking lizardy little man just gave it to me."

She handed it back to me. "Of course," she said. "That's where most people get theirs from."

"From Stelly?"

"Who? I meant from some little Cypriot guy. That's always the story."

"I didn't ask for it. It's really not my thing."

The woman shrugged – I got the feeling she didn't believe me, or that she didn't care. She spoke with a south London accent, but I wouldn't have pinned her as English had I seen her from afar, with her high cheek bones and dark rings around her eyes. She looked to be in her late twenties or maybe a few yards longer than that, dark hair in a ponytail. It didn't even occur to me at first that she worked there – she was not in the pseudo-Roman staff uniform, but a black polo neck and short denim skirt. I protested further that the pill was not mine, and she made a gesture, both with her eyes and her hand to the rest of the club, and suddenly it seemed lighter, and I could see so many more figures than before, and now they looked wild, wild-featured, wild-eyed, and they seemed to bend into one another, dancing, conversing. "Everybody's on something, mate," she said. "I wouldn't get hung up about it if I were you." And she picked the empties up from the bar and passed me, and the dark seemed to fall back down over everyone and she was gone.

I felt heady, and the music thumped and I needed air. I ordered another drink and went back up to find Illie was sitting where I had left him, only now he was with Tara.

"You came back," Illie laughed. "I believe you know Tara."

I sat down heavily. "This place is intense," I said. "I didn't think you two knew each other."

"Oh, darling," Tara said. "We just met."

Somehow I didn't believe her. I was losing count of my drinks as another round turned up from the waiter.

"We were reminiscing about Francis," Illie said.

"And who would have thought we came here for the first time when the island was whole," Tara said. They were talking like old friends, both of them quite drunk.

"When it was whole?" I said.

"Pre-seventy-four," Tara said. "That's when I was first here.

And Illie too. I tell that to Furkan – I was here before you were born, I say to him."

"And he finds that funny?" I said.

"Oh, Furkan adores me, of course he finds it funny."

Illie and Tara shared a joke I didn't catch from under the music and they laughed and rocked in their pews for a little while. Across the way I saw the glass collector from the lower level, doing her glass collecting, and we caught each other's eye and she smiled at me and I found myself smiling back and once again I wondered just what the hell kind of place I had gotten myself into.

I spent the rest of the night keeping an eye out for Stelly and pretending I could hear Tara's jokes above the music. Illie, I am certain, was also humouring her toward the end. But I did not see Stelly again – I wondered if he might crop up in my nightmares. As we were about to leave – Illie offered for me to stay longer, but I said I was very much ready to go – the glass collector appeared at my side once more.

"I wanted to apologise," she said.

"What for?" I said.

"I think I was rude earlier," she said. "I suggested you were just like everyone else, and I've been watching you and it's obvious that's not the case. I'm sorry."

"I'm flattered you've been watching me," I said.

Now she was talking to me directly, rather than superficially as she had done on the lower level, I became aware how attractive she was, with her dark eyes and freckled nose.

"So you'll take me out?" she said, straight up. I didn't know what to say. "No strings," she said, and smiled. "It's just the same old same old out here, and it would be nice to make a new friend who's a bit different from the normal lot."

"This is a *normal* lot?" I said.

She smiled and looked around. "I've been here six months," she said. "Feels like six years. Sixty years."

"So you'd better take me out, then. Show me around."

Her name was Lou. Not Louise. Just Lou. She said surnames were for another island. And we agreed to meet. And that was that. Illie slept on the drive home. I thought of Clare and how I had to call her to make sure she had received the money transfer. But it could wait until morning, I thought. There was so much that could wait until morning.

Eight

"Yes, I received the money," Clare said.

"I appreciate it may have been something of a surprise to see it there in black and white."

"Yes," she said. Her voice was soft, as if distracted by some larger cosmic questions that were never going to be answered in a telephone conversation. "Y'know, it's obvious you're not telling me everything," she went on. "And the tragedy could well turn out to be I don't really care about that."

So there we were, I with motives that grew less selfish the less I loved her, and her with something similar going on.

I had woken that morning in Francis's armchair and the stale smell of his unclean pipe would not leave my nostrils, no matter how far away from the spot I moved. I went down to the pool, and the girls were down there. Dina swam, whilst Darya, the elder, read a book on the lounger. Their father was nowhere to be seen. I stood a few steps up from the poolside for a moment, wondering about the appropriateness of me being there without their father.

"Don't you girls ever leave this pool?" I said, as lightly in tone as I could.

Darya didn't look up from her book, but Dina perched her forearms on the curb of the pool, flattened back her hair and swiped the water from her eyes and nose and mouth. "This is good as nobody can see the pool from the road," she said.

"Dina!" reprimanded Darya.

"Sorry," said Dina, and she rolled her eyes and spun into a backstroke, kicking off from the pool wall with her feet.

"You don't want to be seen from the road?" I said, putting my towel on the lounger a safe few yards from Darya.

"She doesn't mean that," Darya said.

"So what does she mean?"

"She is shy. *Painfully* shy."

I looked up and around, and realised the only place really to view the pool area was from the ridge or from the house. Otherwise it was secluded on all sides.

"Where is your father?" I asked.

"Off doing whatever it is that keeps him busy through the days."

Without Evgeny here, Darya was much more womanly, and the family unit seemed much more of a performance. She did not look up from her paperback. Almost on cue, Evgeny came down the steps in shorts, linen shirt and aviators – he looked like a movie star at Cannes.

"Ah, my friend," he said as he reached the bottom steps, "you are nursing a hangover, I hear?"

"I wouldn't put it quite like that."

I wanted to tell him I had not gotten in the pool as his young daughter was in it, and I felt it would be inappropriate, and somehow gain his respect. How strange a person can be led to act when living with gangsters.

"I always find a swim is the best thing to turn vodka into energy," Evgeny said, and began to strip to his trunks. "Have you seen Illie today? He's been looking for you."

"I haven't left the tower," I said.

"Sometimes he goes down to the wood and forgets," said Darya.

Evgeny gave her a look, not a hard one, but one that pulled her back.

It was at this point I decided to try something out that had been playing on my mind. "I was thinking," I said, "if you don't mind me being so forward – but as I am new to this little set-up, and it

73

looks like we may bump into each other quite a bit, if we could be friends?"

Evgeny prepared to dive into the pool, wrapping his toes around the edge and bending over double.

"You British are so strange," he said, and sprung outstretched into the water.

"I think it's a nice idea," said Dina, once again her head poking out from the water and resting on her forearms at the poolside.

"We're not really supposed to," Darya said. I had noticed she had waited until Evgeny was submerged before she spoke.

"I don't see what harm it would be," I said. "You must have gotten along well with Francis. He always had a warm spot for the family atmosphere."

"We rarely saw him," Darya said.

"Really?" I said.

Evgeny had swum a length straight off the dive and came up at the very far end of the pool. Dina had not moved as a bobbing head.

"He stayed in the tower," Darya said.

"The whole time?" I kept the tone as light as I could.

"All I know is we didn't see much of him."

"We've seen more of you already," Dina said.

"In the last few days, do you mean?"

Dina dunked her head.

"We have seen more of you in the last few days than in the whole time Francis was here," Darya said.

Evgeny came up again, having swum the length back. "Francis had been here a long time before us," he said. "Illie would say he was 'in the zone'."

"What does that mean?"

"The painting," said Evgeny. "He just used to sit in the tower and paint."

74

Nine

I had begun to wonder if it would actually happen, if the job of
work would come to fruition, or if my job was to occupy the
tower as a figure for Illie to view at a distance and convince
himself Francis had never left. I had questioned this idea that
Francis had, by the end of his life at least, locked himself in this
small circular brick tower, and painted as if it was his final chance
to speak his mind in the heart of a burning city. He had described
life to me this way once. "That is why the image of Nero fiddling
while Rome was ablaze is such a powerful one – of course we
think he is mad for doing so, but also in our unconscious we
realise that we are all doing the same." But where were his
paintings? He had been prolific in his youth, before he had settled
as an academic; before he was thirty-five he had thousands of
works to his name. If the finiteness of life is what gives us impetus
to create, then surely we would create more as the end point edges
inevitably closer with time? Who had taken the paintings?

These questions were growing in my mind, to the point where
they were beginning to drown out anything else that may have
been useful to me in that place. And then Illie was at the door, in
moccasins, loose linen trousers and hooded training top. His eyes
were sunken, half-closed, and he wore half-moon reading
spectacles at the end of his short nose. He leaned on the
doorframe, and I saw a bottle of vodka swing in his hand. "I need
you to paint," he said.

I sat upright in the chair and said, "I am ready when you are,
Illie."

He came in – he walked with the drunken swagger of a man who confidently stomped around on hot coals when pissed. It was that measured dangerousness that I must admit I found attractive in the hard-bitten drinking classes. If he had gone the other way, and been a bad drunk, a sloppy emotional drunk, I don't think I could have stayed.

He swung the bottle at me with a pendulous arm, and smiled like Lucifer. I took it and necked a slug. It was hard and clean and burned like pepper.

"You know about light, don't you?" Illie said.

I changed mind-set quickly. This was a serious Illie, one I had not yet seen in full flow. That smile had been a loosener, an introduction.

"Light will be important," he said. He stomped over to the canvases stacked against the wall and picked out a medium-sized one and brought it over to the easel. "Perhaps start with this one." And he gave me a smile. "I don't want you to feel pressure," he said. "My needs are substantial, but I have learned to understand just how delicate you artists are, and that you are fine machines and need to be treated like a Ferrari or a musket. It is no good to rush the thing. Or to allow it to go rusty."

"I'm not rusty," I said.

"No, I caught you just in time, I think. No?"

He slapped me across the shoulder. Hard. He pushed the bottle back up toward his lips.

"Illie, you said something to me the other day, and I have struggled to decipher exactly what it is you meant."

He looked at me with a hard puzzlement.

"You said you wanted me to paint your dreams."

He shrugged. "I speak sometimes like a poet."

I exhaled without meaning to. "Thank goodness," I said. "So you meant that you hope I can create something which speaks to you of something inside of you?"

"Continue," he said.

"We all have dreams, hopes, aspirations. You want me to express something within you. I can see how Francis would have found something very important in that project. He often spoke of the universal truths within us as individuals."

"He did," Illie solemnly nodded. He swigged again and then passed me the bottle. "I miss him," he said. "To lost friends." And he took another swig and handed back to me to repeat, which I did. When I had drank, and finished wincing at the burn, he said, "But that is not it."

"No?"

"I have a recurring dream."

The slugs of vodka were beginning to make Illie's words move more slowly from my ear to my brain.

"You have a recurring dream?"

"Yes. Francis spent years attempting to illustrate it so that I might make sense of it. And I have been searching for it for a decade or more."

"Since your wife died?"

Illie curled his bottom lip and rotated his neck. "Maybe a bit longer. It would be wrong to use her death as an excuse. There comes a time in a man's life when he starts looking back, and realises it is no good to forget, no good to close things off. You know, don't you, how wonderful it is to *feel* something?"

"To feel something?"

"Yes, I mean *anything*. Even the worst things. To feel is to live."

I was going along with this, perhaps because of the vodka, perhaps because I had no other direction to go. "This recurring dream makes you feel something?"

"I think it is the key," he said.

"A key to what?"

He looked at the canvas on the easel and rubbed his hand across his face in a gesture of awakening. "It is night, but not a usual night. The light is silver, purple, grey, blue. It is heavy. The air is heavy."

I stood abruptly and began rifling through Francis's paints and brushes, and picked up an old palette board and squirted globules of paint onto it. I encouraged Illie to continue as I mixed quickly. I felt an unusual surge of energy as he went on, and I began dancing in front of the canvas and dashing great streaks of my mixtures onto the surface.

"No, no, no," Illie said. "Silver and blue and grey and purple and it all folds out of this deep dark night."

"You are a poet, Illie," I laughed, but he did not laugh with me and he just kept saying over and over again, blue and purple and grey and silver, and it grew into a shout, and I mixed more and more and scratched down the canvas and streaked across it with different shades and different hues, and it felt exciting, the two of us in this strange embrace.

And then his shouting turned into a whip-sharp bark. "No," he said. I stopped and turned to him, the energy pulled out of me like a cord. "You are missing what I am saying. Where is the weight? The heaviness? I cannot get that from some stripes on a white sheet."

I looked at the canvas, and then at Illie, who was swigging once more from the now nearly-empty bottle.

"It is early days," he said. "But I cannot know you have got the picture correct until I see the entire thing."

Once again I looked at the canvas and then at Illie. I had been breathing heavily, excitedly, and now it was subduing back to normal.

"You want me to paint the whole thing and then you tell me if I have it right or not?"

"Yes, that is correct."

"The whole thing."

"Yes, the entire painting."

78

"Of this darkness."

"The silver, purple, blue…"

"…blue, grey. Yes, I got that."

"And in the middle of it is a swing."

He made a swinging motion with his arms.

"A swing?" I said.

"A child's swing," he said. "From a playground. In the middle. Well, not quite in the middle, it is a little off to the left sometimes. And as I walk up to it, it becomes more central. A little red swing under the cover of a tree. A tree with naked branches."

"What kind of tree, Illie?" I said.

And he looked up at me from his seat on the footstool, the bottle now empty in his hand, and he shrugged, and he said, "I'll know it when I see it."

79

Ten

My hands ached, and they were scarred with deep impressions of purple and black paint. I woke and my fingers were stiff and curved like claws. It was like being a child again, my fingers bent with the memory of an energy that ignores physical restrictions and the poor humanness of muscle.

I climbed down from the mezzanine in the tower, my head splitting. I was out of practise when it came to it – the painting if not so much the drinking. I realised there was something in what Clare said about my fire dimming. (She never put it quite so cuttingly, but this is what she was getting at.) But the truth was, take away the crooked mouth of my hangover and I felt like I'd lost my virginity, like the world was new.

The ground floor of the tower was a bombsite, with artists' paraphernalia the rubble. I remembered Illie's face being close to mine, his hands cupping my ears, those piercing blue eyes of his – he reminded me of one of those photographs of Picasso in old age that made him look half-psychotic – and he was screaming into my face, "Deeper red, deeper red."

I filled the sink with cold water and plunged my head into it. The sharp shock that went up my neck and over my spine jolted me halfway back to normality. I made coffee on the little stove, and quickly ate some of the stale bread I had left. Something was deterring me from going over to the house for a real breakfast. I wondered how often Francis had woken in this state and gone straight back to the brandy. I looked at that bottle on the table next to the armchair for a while, testing myself. The longer I looked the more nauseous I felt.

Eventually, I went over to the house, tiptoed through the kitchen and through the silence and I found the telephone and called the number Lou (not Louise) – the waitress from The Castle – had given me a few nights before. She answered with a sprightly tone, but as soon as she got talking I could tell it was her – flat vowels and a worldly pitch. As luck would have it she had the day off work and could meet me in an hour or so.

I found Viktor in his shirt sleeves waxing the Bentley, and he said he would drive me to Napa on condition I didn't tell Illie, and that he had not seen Illie since the day before anyway, not since before he came to the tower to see me. If I was concerned for Illie, it came second to getting out of that place, to being by the beach, to having strangers stroll by and noise go on around me. And to seeing Lou, of course. My mood was for company.

I met her in The White Bar, where she was drinking a neon green virgin cocktail at the bar, chatting familiarly with the girl serving. Lou looked different to how I remembered her – women always do in the light of day. She was perhaps younger than the thirty-something I had her down for, but the sun had dried her skin and fired bleached streaks through her brown hair. She was shorter than I remembered, more attractive, perhaps because of her relaxed shoulders and the way she leaned back and put her sandaled foot up on the neighbouring stool.

"You look like you've had a rough night," she said, and she half-smiled. I looked down over myself, and I realised how dishevelled I was. But she pointed out she was referring to my paint-stained hands. "You see some catastrophes in this place, especially in my line of work, but what exactly have you been up to?"

"Work," I said.

"Somebody has you painting fences?"

"Something like that."

She sucked long on the straw of her drink as my own cocktail was served up. I copied her, and winced at the sharpness of the citrus fruits before it levelled out as the sugar hit.

"I'm hungover too," she said.

"How come you look so much better than me?" I said.

"It's all about confidence," she said. "And these." She tapped the side of the glass.

She hopped from the stool and we went and sat out on the veranda looking down over the streets leading to the big beach hotels, and then out to the sea. Lou lowered her shades that had been tucked onto the top of her head and made herself very small on a seat up close to the picket fencing that lined the parameter of the veranda.

"So you came out here to do odd jobs?" she said.

"Not my initial plan." I looked down guiltily at my blackened hands. "Did you come out here to wait tables?"

"I came out here to get away from my boyfriend," she said. "Ex-boyfriend. He was my ex when I left and he's even more my ex now. Waiting tables is what everyone does."

"You don't seem the type to do what everyone does."

"This is the only place I have ever been where nobody has any money and nobody ever bitches about it. We all just go through the day to day, get fucked up, go to work, sit in the sun, go for a swim. Trust me, you have never been to a more couldn't-give-a-fuck place in your life."

"And you have no plans to leave?"

"Plans are another thing that get forgotten out here. All over the place you'll meet with people who once had lives like yours. And now it's all just something else. There's a guy – Kenny – works in the Irish bar down the road – he must have been here thirty years pulling fucking pints in that place. He's not doing it for the final salary pension, I can assure you. People find different ways to live out their lives. It's an island thing, sure, but it's also something to do with *this* island."

"Traps come in all shapes and sizes," I said.

She blew a raspberry at me and slumped back in her chair. "People come here thinking they can make money. They come here thinking this is rich pickings for the right type of arsehole. You can make a few hundred thousand maybe, if you're ruthless, but not millions. These guys make the mistake thinking this is some kind of playground, but it's not; it's a waiting room, a lost space. And they always get found out. You have to remember Cyprus is like a little hub for fucking arseholes. You go in every direction off the edge of this island and you'll find the edge of a massively corrupt gangster state."

"You don't talk like a waitress," I said.

Lou laughed. "Waitressing is the new front line intelligence service in this part of the world. It used to be telephony, fifty years ago or so – you know, the women who connect your call and then could just listen in? They always sounded robotic, but they were for hire to any nation or ideologue that was ready to pay."

We looked across at each other for a moment. I couldn't tell just how serious she was being. And then she laughed.

"Are you working for some clandestine agency?" I said.

She laughed again. "Nobody has offered the right money. Yet." And she arched her eyebrows.

"Do you know Illie Prostakov? The guy I was in The Castle with the other night?"

"The old guy? I've seen him around. I know he's one of the VIPs. We're supposed to make sure he is well looked after. Is it him you're working for?"

"Strange how things have worked out," I said. "He's a bit messed up."

Lou rolled her eyes. "Fuck, they all are. These guys you see walking around with their chests puffed out, looking all mean and dangerous, they all go home and cry, wanking into a watermelon. It's all children's games, and normal people like you

83

and me get caught up in it, because like toddlers they have managed to make everything about them. It's money of course. But even in Napa where there is none, they've made it look like they have it, so we all follow them around."

"You think Illie is like that?"

"Is he broke? I have no idea. I don't know him. But he's lonely, I know that much. Probably why he hired you."

"He's not lonely," I said, mixing the last inch of the drink with the crushed ice at the bottom of the glass. It had indeed done remarkable things for the hangover. "He's not alone," I said. "He has family staying with him."

Lou curled her bottom lip and thought about this for a moment. "He didn't seem like a family guy," she said.

"Oh, I don't think they're all that close. He doesn't seem to dote on them or anything. But they've come to stay with him and have been up at the house for months, so far as I can tell."

"I've never seen him with anyone in the club."

"I don't think they get out much." I waved to the passing waitress and gestured for two more of the same. "But you know what teenage girls are like," I said.

"So, they're his granddaughters or something?"

"I don't know what they are. Grand-nieces or something, maybe? I'm surprised they haven't hit the town, but they seem quite content up there at the house sitting by the pool." There was a long thoughtful pause from Lou. "I'm just saying, I don't quite think Illie fits in with your theory of Russians in Cyprus."

"There are always exceptions," she said, and waved a sarcastic finger at me. "Shall we drink these and then go for a swim?" she said.

"I don't have any swimming gear with me," I said.

She laughed. "Neither do I," she said.

We actually had two more drinks. The sun was crisp and the rays were absolute, and, as Lou warned, the hangover cures worked so well that by the time we were ready for a swim we instead moved on to non-virgin cocktails. Lou talked about her upbringing, although always in sweeping terms, never anecdotes about school or her parents, but rather in surprisingly circumspect and philosophical abstractions. "Parents are supposed to firm you up, and they can do this by either pressing at you constantly with their hands, or letting it all hang out and seeing how the wind blows. And mine were more of the second type." "I hate to sound like a dropout philosopher, waiting tables in Napa and acting like I have it all figured out, but school is designed to provide corporations with employees, and that's all. If you want to not waste your life you have to reject school and everything it has to offer. I'd read more books than all of my teachers combined by the time I was fourteen, and I'm a better person for having failed my exams twice over." "Growing up is the purest thing a person will ever do – and once you're all grown, it's your societal duty to batter the purity out of the next generation coming behind you. It's conditioning. Much more powerful than indoctrination. It's not about politics, it's about a conviction that this is what the human condition *is*, naturally, and there's no way – and no reason – to fight it."

It was hard to disagree that Lou was twice as interesting as anyone I had met back home with their university degrees tucked into their belts. And the uncanny thing was, there were moments when she sounded like Francis, and other moments when she sounded like Clare.

We ate seafood down on Nissi Beach as the sun dipped into the water. By the end of the evening, I felt as though I had known Lou much longer than just a day, and yet on reflection I had learned very little about her biography, and a lot about her world view. Her father had been in the army and so as a child she had travelled a great deal, but this titbit just served to lead into a mystical treatise on the life of the itinerant, which is how she saw herself – a nomad. "I'm one of life's grazers; but I suppose we can afford to be when we're young. The trick is to reach the end chapter and not be imprisoned."

The only skag in this day of soul food was when Lou went to the Ladies and all of a sudden I felt the seedy presence of Stelly on the beach. The sun was all but gone now, and the vista was a burnt amber and black-blues, and there he was, heading for me, bobbing in that dreadful way of his – although he didn't look at me once, and could have been walking anywhere on the large and busy beach, I knew he was coming to me. And he was. Instead of a word of hello he came up close and nodded his head, his whole body motion dancing to a silent beat that went on somewhere in that ugly head of his. He was his usual self, unblemished by the threat of bathing, a change of attire (still just shorts and cap), or a scrubbing away of that strong smell of his – not disgusting, like a Soho tramp, but a heavy natural oily smell of sweat, of smoke, of leather. I wondered if he woke in a cave at sunset and slipped across the rocks to do whatever it was that was on his mind.

"You take my gift?" he said, his narrow eyes now fixed on me. His eyes had no colour, no white, as I remember, they were just the dark slits of a blind reptile.

"If you mean that pill you gave me, I didn't take it. Not my thing."

He bobbed on the balls of his feet.

"I couldn't find you," he said.

"I went home," I said.

"With that Ruski?"

"Yes."

He smiled that awful ashy smile. "So you fuck? That the deal?"

"That's not the deal," I said.

He nodded, both unconvinced and disinterested. And then he looked back at me, and like a predator about to strike his eyes opened from their cocoons and the whites came out, then the pink irises, and he said, "He found his treasure yet?"

I wasn't quite sure what he said. "What did you say?"

"That Russian. Had that old English making maps for him. He dead now, the English? The painter?"

"That's right."

We stared at each other.

"You keep the pill," Stelly said, and slowly began to bob away from me in the sand. "A gift," he said. I was glad – as I imagined was the case for everyone – that he was gone. And he knew what he was doing, this weasel, you could see it in his eyes, in that strange arrogant expression on his face, the slits of his eyes, the thinness of his lips.

Lou returned. "What's wrong?" she said, noticing the change in my demeanour.

"Stelly," I said.

She affected a shiver down the spine.

"That creepy bastard. Was he here? Good job you didn't take that pill he gave you the other night."

"Not my thing," I said.

"No, but apparently he has a thing for drugging guys and then fucking them in the back lanes."

That pricked up my ears. "He *rapes* them?"

And Lou raised her eyebrows, as if to say, *yes*, but she said, "This is Cyprus, mate; they don't really go in for labels like that. Just stay the fuck away from him."

I tried to forget about him, but it lingered. As much what he said about Illie's *treasure* as what Lou said about him. I had wanted to bring up the notion of the treasure with Lou, but it seemed absurd, despite the absurdity of it all. The whole island was absurd. For the first time since arriving I thought of getting out. Lou noticed the change in my mood, and she offered to take me to another bar, or perhaps back to her place to talk more, for some relative quiet. The idea of going back to Lou's digs – and she explained that although she had her own place, it was in a complex of hardworking, hard-partying Napa club and bar staff – made me think of the entire day in a different light.

Had I been wanting something to happen between Lou and I? Had that been what *she* wanted? Had some part of my mind already decided that me and Clare were over – because that is how it happens, isn't it; one day you notice your chemical self has made the decision to leave and informs your public self of the way things are going to play out. I was sure Clare was going through similar phases back home. But my intention was never to fuck things up in this way. Adultery was something Francis would never have approved of – he had famously railed against such goings on, even in the height of his bohemian period after the war. Lou and I embraced at the entrance to the alley that led to her complex. We were both more than a little pissed by now. We kissed on the mouth, and it felt like a test run, to see if we could both get through some kind of earthly barrier, and I understood as we connected that she had some barriers of her own that stemmed from that abstract biography of hers. We smiled at each other, embraced again, and I said, "I would really like to do this again." Instead of closing down as I expected her to, she said, "And so would I."

I watched her walk down the alley and then turn a corner out of sight, and it was then I realised I was going to have to somehow find my way back to Illie's without any idea of where it really was. As I was scratching my head about this, I noticed the silhouette of a familiar figure down the end of the street. It was Viktor, and he waved his arm at me slowly, perhaps reluctantly.

"He's been wondering where you've been," he said as we walked to the car.

"And what did you say?"

"I said you had wanted some fresh air so I drove you to the beach up at Cape Greco. He won't take kindly to hearing you were in Napa."

"Have you been trailing me all day?" I said.

"You didn't stray far," Viktor said. "You didn't tell her anything about Illie, did you?" he said, gesturing toward the entrance to the alley Lou had gone up with a nod of his head. "Or Evgeny and the girls?"

"No, not at all," I said.

The lie was stupid. It felt stupid as it came out of my mouth, and there was no doubt Viktor had recognised it for a lie. The drive back to Illie's happened in silence.

Eleven

The second painting session started out quite differently from the first. Illie again appeared at the door of the tower – I was reading in the armchair – and this time he was sober and dressed in that moneyed smart-casual way. His Picasso eyes were not burning so brightly as they had done last time – there was something of the jovial Illie I had come to know about him now.

"We have not seen each other in a few days," he said. "You are good?"

"Yes," I said.

"Viktor tells me he took you into town."

I nodded.

Illie stepped inside slowly, casting an admiring eye around the interior of the place as if he had never set foot in there before. "It is good that you are making yourself feel at home. But perhaps in future you could tell me before you go off."

"I didn't know I was a prisoner."

"How very dramatic of you," Illie said. "I am merely pointing out that in some ways now you live on my property I am responsible for you. You see the position that puts me in, do you not?"

I did not, and I also did not trust his sincerity in the reasoning, but I was not going to push it. "Of course," I said.

"Good." He smiled widely, his brow arched into a charming bow. "Also I cannot have you just running off with Viktor. I am responsible for him too, you know?"

"Yes," I said. "I am sorry."

Illie puffed and waved his hand dismissively, still walking around the perimeter of the tower and acting as though he was admiring the décor.

"You have painted more since we last were together?"

I said that I had not. He nodded, curling that lip in the way that suggested he was unhappy with the answer.

"What are you reading?" he said.

"*Treasure Island*," I said. "An old copy was in the bedside drawer. Francis must have left it here. It's funny, but I don't think I've ever read it. Not properly. I think maybe I had a picture book version when I was a kid."

"I am paying you a lot of money," Illie said. "But not so you can read *Treasure Island*."

He spoke softly, without any hint of menace, but it was there, as if I had created the threat for myself out of the subtleties. I had closed the book some time ago, but now I placed it on the table.

I stood and grabbed a brush and a canvas from the stack by the wall. "You're quite right, Illie," I said. "I have been raising the white flag since that somewhat exhausting session the other day." I placed the canvas forcefully onto the easel. "What is it you need from me today?"

Illie looked at me – his eyes had deadened – and then he looked at the canvas, and then back at me. His shoulders hunched.

"The same," he said.

"The same?"

"Yes. Well, not quite. Because you got it wrong the other night. Over and over, you got it wrong."

"So what is the same?" I said, my hand, holding the brush, dropping to my side.

"The dream is the same. The night is the same. The swing is still that deep sweet red."

I had suspected Illie's madness, but this felt close to home, as if it now was also partly my madness, that he had forced it on me and I had nothing left to fight back.

"You want me to paint the same painting I painted the other day?"

"Yes," said Illie with an expressionless, flat face. "*That* is the work."

"Over and over?"

"Until you get it right."

"Until I recreate what it is you see in your head?"

"That is correct."

His eyes moved from me to the canvas and then back again, as if he could not quite figure out why I was asking questions and not getting on with the job at hand.

I had not intended to ask any question relating to what Stelly had told me, partly because I felt Stelly was as trustworthy as the devil himself. But it had nagged at me – probably exactly what he had intended. I turned to the tools of my trade, such as they were, and spoke with my back to Illie as I began to mix colours on the palette.

"What is it you're looking for?" I said.

"What do you mean?"

"Having me do this – and this is what you had Francis doing, I take it?"

"I have been very lucky that you came here to his funeral and were able to take his place."

"But you are looking for something, aren't you?"

Illie was silent behind me. I applied the first colour to the brush and began to paint the night.

"Darker," he said. "You fail to catch the silver. It must be darker."

Twelve

I had no intention of becoming Illie's prisoner, of finding myself in some way akin to Evgeny and his girls, living by the pool for the rest of their lives. When I approached Viktor with a reasonable idea – that he would allow me to take the old green Hyundai that I had seen tucked away at the back of the garage, a few times a week, then I would promise to be discreet and not to get him into trouble – it seemed possible that he had a similar arrangement with Francis. He nodded as if he knew the drill.

"And what about Dina and Darya? Do they ever borrow this car?"

Viktor frowned and shook his head. "Nobody has driven it since Mr Benthem was alive. In fact, Mr Prostakov asked me to get rid of it. He thinks it is an abomination of the automotive art."

"Do the girls ever leave?"

Viktor just stared at me. One question too many.

I took the keys from his hand and was off to Napa. I had been thinking about Lou – she had been there in my mind during all these strange days – her laconic island wisdom, her energising take on life. I drove straight to her complex.

I knocked on several doors, not knowing which room was hers, but after the third or fourth she answered, and was surprised to see me, a surprise that seemed to melt into something like welcome.

"You have a car?" she said.

She left me at the door, saying her room was hardly fit for drop-in guests, and came back a moment later with her purse and sunglasses.

"I'm going to take you sightseeing," she said with a playful poke to my breastplate, and led me back down to the street.

We drove for a few hours, and I was already wondering if I was on course to retreat on my promise to Viktor of only being gone a short while. Lou would not tell me exactly where she was directing me, but she said several times how this had been such a good day to surprise her. A clear day.

"I haven't known any other type of day since I've been here," I said.

"Ah, yes, there's clear, and then there's *clear*," and she tapped her temple with her forefinger. "Not had a drink since I saw you last, and I have a few days off work. I'm detoxed, focussed." She pointed histrionically out toward the road.

Before long the secret destination became more difficult to hide from me, as we drove into the foothills of the Troodos Mountains.

"From the highest peak you can see the entire island," Lou said.

"The entire island?" I said incredulously. But Lou just nodded with a satisfied smile on her face.

As we went further into the territory the countryside became lusher; woodland began to bristle up at the roadside and create dense avenues. Lou continued to direct with curious accuracy, as if it was all second nature, and we turned on to the road to Mount Olympus.

"This isn't *the* Mount Olympus?" I said, showing my ignorance of the classical world. "The one where the gods lived?"

"No. Although I think Aphrodite was born around here somewhere."

"So it's the island of love?" I said.

"She was an outsider," Lou said. "Like everyone else on Cyprus."

The day was indeed clear, and as we rose through the wooded roads that curled like whip marks up the mountain sides we passed several villages clinging to the sides of the valleys, and then signs for ski resorts – there were four on Olympus, Lou informed me – and signs for restaurants and hotels. But amongst these were also abandoned huts and villas peeking out from behind trees deeper into the woods. The heat cleared out, the air thinned, the car felt like it was gliding.

It was a long drive and we passed many cars on the way, including some military vehicles. On reaching the peak, which housed a car park and a vantage balcony for the public, I could see more military vehicles, a checkpoint and armed guards near a fence.

"What is all this?" I said.

We pulled further up toward the car park and there I could see a compound of several windowless concrete buildings positioned around a huge white dome.

"It's the military radar station," Lou said. "Nothing to be worried about. It's British, I think. Keeping an eye on the Turks."

I pulled up in a bay and we got out of the car. Despite the promise – which I assumed to be an exaggeration – I was surprised by the image of the sea, distant across the horizon like a celeste ribbon.

"Told you," Lou said. "Two thousand metres up gets you quite a view."

"Hence the radar," I said. Now giving the military complex a little more attention I could see armed guards casually patrolling inside the fence, and then in my eye-line I could see another, smaller complex on a neighbouring peak. Lou noticed my preoccupation.

"You come across things like this here," she said.

"What do you mean?"

"Military presence. Obviously the British have their feet in the door, but then the Cypriots down this half of the island are very wary of the Turks."

I put my hand up to my eyes to shield the sun. There was some serious kit up on these mountains, or at least somebody wanted to give the impression of serious kit. It was on display for every tourist who went up there. And even with my poor knowledge of Cyprus's history, I could spot such posturing a mile off. The Turkish invasion in 'seventy-four had been known as something of a bloodless revolution, with reporters walking with the Turkish soldiers, interviewing them as they stuffed away their parachutes. There had been chaos, but not much of a fight. All this looked like a defiant gesture of work unfinished on the part of the invaded nation.

"They have it pretty easy here," Lou said. "If you think Cyprus is almost Africa." She pointed south. "It's almost Europe." She spun and pointed north. "And it's almost the Middle East." She turned again and pointed east, out over the vast unmade bed of mountains and, it seemed, out to the sprawling flatlands of Cyprus that disappeared into a pattern of miniscule patchworks. The view went further than my eyes could see.

"You can see Napa," Lou said, pointing.

I squinted. "Where?"

"See the sea?" She pointed with a little extra verve. "Right out there."

"Sure." I thought perhaps I could see some darkening at the furthest reaches.

"And inland there you can see the island go to the north," Lou said. "Have you ever seen such a view?"

"The air is thin up here," I said.

"Feeling a bit light-headed?" Lou ribbed. She wrapped her arms around my arm and held close to me. She wore a warm, free smile. "I love it up here," she said. "Down there it's a crazy island, but from up here it's immortal, isn't it?"

There were others at the peak: sightseers, tourists, as well as the guards over the way at the complex. A young couple took photographs of each other in turn with their backs to the view. Another couple with a young boy tucked into packed sandwiches handed out by the mother from a picnic box placed on the bonnet of their car. But it was quiet, not shut-down quiet, but wide-open quiet, as if all the smallest noises of the world, like men speaking and car engines revving, had been sucked up into the glorious eternal vastness of the world. From up there the island seemed to breathe like a sleeping giant in the sun.

"Can you see the wall?" Lou said. She was pointing into the blindness of extreme distance once again, out past the dark shade she had assured me was Ayia Napa. I could see nothing but the fading haze of the island.

"What wall am I looking for?" I said, squinting once again.

"The demarcation zone," she said.

I did not know what she was referring to.

"I don't know what it is I'm supposed to be looking for," I said.

"Okay, well, it's hardly visible from space," Lou said, and she marched back to the car and came back with her handbag, pulling out a pair of binoculars as she returned.

"You have binoculars?" I said, surprised.

"But be careful with them," she said handing them to me. "They may think we're spies."

Lou grabbed me by the elbow and ran me over to a more secluded spot, behind a man-moved boulder at the edge of the peak and under the cover of some drooping tree branches.

"I don't want to be arrested as a spy, Lou," I said, trying to unfurl the binocular strap from around my neck. But Lou tugged the strap back down and urged me to look back out over the way.

"You're British, it'll be fine," she said, and she held the lenses up to my eyes.

"Okay, okay, okay. What am I looking at?"

"The wall was put up in 'seventy-four, to separate Greek Cyprus from the Turkish side. Can you see it?"

The binoculars were surprisingly powerful, and I was more sure – although not wholly convinced – that the shadow I had been looking at before *was* Ayia Napa. Limassol, much closer and to the south, was clearly visible with them. Lou took the binoculars without taking the strap from around my neck, tugging me close to her, cheek to cheek, and she focussed back out to the east.

"There," she said, and put them back to my eyes. "The wall."

I could see a thin line of fudged grey that may or may not have been a wall. It was so far away – fifty, sixty miles? "It stretches the length of the island," Lou said. "From north to south. It even cuts towns in half."

"It cuts through Nicosia – is that right?" I knew a little, had read a little.

"That's right." She mock punched me across the shoulder. "Straight through the middle of the capital. People really had a thing for walls in the twentieth century, don't you agree?"

"They do seem old fashioned now," I said.

"That's what this island is all about," Lou laughed. "One day I'll take you to see Famagusta."

"Famagusta? What's that?"

"The abandoned city."

"Quite a melodramatic nickname."

"Not a nickname. It's a ghost town. Cut in two by the wall and abandoned overnight in 'seventy-four. It's like Pompeii, only no ash. Just cars in the roads, streets overgrown. A real zombie apocalypse type place. You can't go in there, but you can look at it. Now *that* is a place you won't be able to take binoculars."

"No?"

"The armed guards aren't protecting anything in Famagusta."

"So what are they doing there?"

"Well, the official line, so I'm told, is something to do with protecting the demarcation zone, but if you go down to the beach you'll see gun turrets, and when they see you, they'll aim at you until you're gone."

"I don't need to go there," I said.

Lou laughed. "They won't *shoot* you. They just want you to know they *see* you."

"It all seems a bit highly-strung."

"Well, that's what I mean. All seems a bit much."

"So what's your conspiracy theory?" I said.

"I wouldn't call it that. Maybe more of an urban myth."

"Go on." We had sunk by this point to sitting on the floor behind the boulder, in total hiding from both tourists and military.

"The story goes that Famagusta was never totally abandoned, and that in actual fact it's become something of a town of robbers and thieves. That's the romantic way of putting it; the children's bedtime story version."

"What's the grown up version?"

"The grown up version is that there is a secret tunnel into Famagusta and the Russian Mafia use it as a hiding place for those most wanted by various authorities."

"Wow," I said. "That is *quite* the urban myth."

Lou got back to her feet and leaned across the boulder with binoculars aimed like an arch-surveillor. "It's eerie as fuck, is all I know," she said.

"You've been?"

"I saw it from the north. All those huge abandoned hotels and holiday resorts. Famagusta was a bit of a gold coast resort in the early 'seventies."

I got up next to her and took the binoculars. I could still only see a faint line that may or may not have been a wall, and nothing resembling an abandoned city.

"Maybe you can see your house from here?" Lou joked.

"You mean my tower," I said.

"Your *tower*?"

"Yes. My own fairy tale castle," I said sarcastically. "I live in a tower near an old forgotten wood, and a swimming pool constantly occupied by an odd motherless Russian family."

"Just the two girls and the dad?"

"Yeah." I lifted the binoculars. "Not sure where it would be from here."

"It can't be that hard to spot. What kind of tower is it?"

"I think it's an old remodelled water tower. Although I'm no expert on these things." She took the binoculars back from me.

"Whereabouts would you say it is? It can't be that hard to spot if there's a tower on the estate."

I was happy to play along, and I began pointing from the half-imagined spots where Napa lay and then where I supposed Paralimni might be. "It would be at a kind of ninety degree apex from these two points." She let out a short sharp gasp and I thought for a moment, unbelievably, that she could see it. "Is that it?" I said. "Surely not."

"No," she said. But she had seen something, she couldn't hide it. I was about to press her, but she took my hand and pulled me back down behind the boulder. I thought she was going to kiss me, our eyes locked for a moment, but she didn't. "I'll need to get back soon," she said after a short while of silence, both of us just soaking up a bit of that sumptuous mountain quiet.

"Sure," I said. "I've had a really nice afternoon." And I had meant it.

"Me too," she said.

We stopped for half an hour for some coffee and cake on the way back down the mountain, and the whole place was beginning to feel less and less Mediterranean and more Appalachian or something like that – firs and chipmunks and picnic benches. Lou laughed and she elaborated on stories of the Russian Mafia and its ties to the "Famagusta tunnel", and how the armed guards were actually hunting for signs of criminal gangs hiding away. But she said, without laughing, that there were also stories of some people living in Famagusta who had never left, they had refused to abandon their homes.

"People would surely know that though," I said. "I mean, you couldn't hide for thirty years in an abandoned town, especially if the military were looking for you."

"I don't know," said Lou. "As I say, this is a crazy island. What you see is more than you can possibly understand, and you don't see the half of it."

Thirteen

As I dropped Lou back off at her digs, I found myself telling her that I wished to see her again. I had to trust myself that I didn't sound romantic, but I may have done. I called Clare when I got back to the house but there was no answer and the message I left her was perfunctory – *Just checking in, hope everything is good with you, will call tomorrow*.

However, when I went to call at Lou's room the next day – we arranged to get some food in Napa before she started work – there was no answer there either. I persisted, peeked through the slatted window and sought out someone who looked like a janitor and asked for information, but there was none to be had, and so I walked out into the glaring heat of the main drag and decided that rather than return to the tower and the solitude of that strange occupation of mine, I would instead go and amble around in the sun for an hour or two, clear my head.

I walked up the way to Furkan's bar, and there, as I supposed I had half-hoped, was Tara, drinking a stemmed glass of lager in a booth. She had just closed the gallery for the day and was waiting to grab a bite with Furkan. "The Ayia Napa art gallery business affords flexible working hours – what can I say?" She laughed loudly. "Please do join us for food, though, if you're as much the lost little lamb as you look."

I took a seat across from her, although she soon sidled closer to me.

"I was meeting a friend, but I can't find her," I said.

"*Her*?" Tara raised her eyebrows. "You got the hang of Napa quite quick."

"Just a friend," I said, as much to myself as to Tara. "She's been showing me around the island."

"Ah, a local?"

"Not quite. She works tables at The Castle," I said. I ordered a soft drink from the waitress.

"Not drinking?" Tara said.

I shrugged. "A day off it," I said.

"So who's the girl?" Tara put on some kind of Mae West impersonation, dipped her shoulder and cocked her eyebrows.

"We just met the other night when we were there with Illie," I said.

"Ah, yes, the Russian gentleman." Tara's face dropped, the lines that were there to symbolise some innate joy smoothed out. "He's a sad case."

I went for it.

"Tara, forgive me if I speak out of turn, but it didn't seem like that was the first time you and Illie had met the other night."

She thought for a moment.

"Yes," she said. "We know each other. *Used* to know each other. From a long time back. Another life."

"Was it a surprise to see him?"

"It's only recently we've become aware of each other again. And it's difficult." She looked at me for a second with a sad smile. "Both happy and sad. The other night you saw us happy." She took a swig of her beer. "He thinks he's looking for answers when in fact he's just holding off on the inevitable. That's a frustration for me. He has had a happy life, so far as I can tell. Now he wants to mess things up."

"Mess things up?"

"For me, I mean. Our happiness and sadness has overlapped it seems. And he's come back into my world at the exact point when he can ruin everything."

"You mean with Furkan?"

103

Tara sighed.

"Illie is looking for redemption," she said. "He has no interest in me. I need to keep him away from Furkan."

"So you're not his saviour?"

"You don't know? He hasn't told you?"

I shook my head.

"He hasn't changed all that much, then," she said. "Illie doesn't really..." she searched for a word; "...connect with people. People are not flesh and blood, they are a means to an end. He is interested in everything else. Money. Ideas. Religion. But people are too real for him."

"Stelly said something very strange to me," I said, trying to make sense of all this.

Tara's face changed – it went hard and her eyes narrowed. "Well, yes, I warned you about him," she said.

I let it go. I felt stupid for mentioning the lizard's name.

"Why would it be such a disaster for Illie to meet Furkan?" I said. "Is he trying to drive the two of you apart?"

Tara was close to tears now, holding it together.

She seemed to steel herself. "Furkan is one of the Golden Orphans," she said. "It's no secret, but it tends to be something we don't really talk about."

"What do you mean? What is a Golden Orphan?"

She smiled with a motherly tap on my downturned hand. "In nineteen seventy-four, when the Turks invaded, a lot of people were killed. It was under-reported, just how brutal it was, how awful. It was a terrible thing that invasion. One of the upshots was that when the fighting died down and the partition was settled there were thirty babies without parents. *Thirty* babies. Well, the Greek Cypriot government used them as symbols of hope, but also as symbols of horror, to rub the Turkish noses in the unholy fucking mess they had created. But amidst all this, the thirty babies grew to be thirty children, and then thirty adults, and every day they became, more and more, thirty folk heroes."

"And Furkan is one of them?"

Tara nodded solemnly.

"Furkan has tried to do good with this. He has his businesses, but most of what he makes he puts back into the community, and helps out people in need. Others of the thirty did good too. Some not so good. Some did pretty bad."

I looked at Tara's face, and it looked a thing filled with the weight of ancient wisdom at that moment.

"God," I said. Something came to me at that moment, and I'm not sure why, but it seemed something implanted the question in my mouth. "Is Stelly one of them too?"

She looked at me. "Nobody knows *what* Stelly is," she said. But she didn't deny it.

"So what is Illie's interest in these Golden Orphans?" I said.

Tara lit a cigarette. "He wants to meet them," she said. "One by one."

"All of the Golden Orphans?"

"This island is built on legends. Aphrodite rose out of the sea off the coast of Paphos – Cypriots do legends well. So there's nothing to it. But as it goes, the rumour was that there were more than thirty, and that the others hid in what is now the demarcation zone."

"In Famagusta?"

"Thereabouts. But it's all a myth. They call it the ghost town, so I suppose they had to put some ghosts in it."

"But babies?"

"Grew up feral. Quite the bogeyman story."

"I've heard there is a tunnel."

Tara's tears had dried up, and she blew her nose in a paper napkin.

"There's no tunnel," she said. "There's no anything. It's not unusual for people to want to talk to Furkan about these things. There was a time when people used to come to his door with sick family members, for Christ's sake. He was a point of pilgrimage. And that takes its toll. I've known him a long time. He hasn't always been as strong and focussed as he is today."

I thought about this for a second. Tara and Illie, that night in The Castle, had talked about the thing they had in common, that they remembered Cyprus in the days before the invasion and partition.

"Do you mind if I ask: did you know Furkan when he was a baby?"

Tara's eyes fluttered uncomfortably. She took a deep breath. "Life is made up of chapters," she said. "And we fell in love in a very different, much later chapter than the one where we first laid eyes on each other."

A silence came next, and it seemed fitting, not too heavy, but it gave us both some space.

"I think I might have that drink after all," I said, and Tara laughed gently and it cracked through the tension.

I waved at the barkeep for a drink. "I'll join you," Tara said.

Fourteen

Despite any urges I may have had to the contrary, I stuck to just a couple of beers that afternoon. I went back to Lou's digs but she was still nowhere to be seen, so I returned to the house with a renewed sense of curiosity about this whole peculiar island.

I had an answerphone message from Clare that was no less perfunctory than the one I had left for her the day before. She sounded exhausted, but in a different way from the way in which she sounded exhausted around me. She sounded like she was in the process of catching up with her life. She said the money had gone to the correct people, and that she had taken her father out for dinner with a little of what was left over. I was glad she did, I would have said. And then she said that she was not stupid, and that she knew I had debts I had kept from her, and that even though she had thought about it, and her father had outright encouraged it, she had not taken the surplus, but that it was there in our joint savings account, waiting for me to come home and settle up. Before she hung up there was a pause, as if she was going to say something else. But she didn't.

The sun seemed to be setting early, and I went down to the pool to swim a few lengths before dinner. The girls were there, of course; Darya reading and Dina filing her nails, her hair wet and matted from a recent swim. We exchanged pleasantries – even Darya was in a good mood and made a few jokes about how her sister bleached in the sun. I swam my lengths, bade them farewell, and went back to the tower where the latest instalment of a new habit had taken place – my dinner on a trolley under a silver lid complete with chilled wine and carnation in a little porcelain vase. It was both delightful and lonesome.

The dinner was good but I wasn't taking to it, and after a few mouthfuls I pushed the trolley to one side, poured another glass of the excellent wine and turned to face the canvas. I had already noticed that the effort from the previous night had gone. Illie had suggested I might find this to be the case from time to time. His plan – which he would not explain – could not wait for my permission. And besides, the paintings were *his*. He made that clear.

I mixed on the palette, scraped the blue grey black with the knife across the surface. It looked no different to the one before, the one that Illie had said was no good. He had said he wanted the right feeling, the right atmosphere, that there must be the whiff of smoke to the hue. I had already stopped pleading with him for clearer direction. I had stopped telling him that it would be impossible to see into his mind and pick out his dreams, because it was impossible to look at a dream even when it was your own. The mad man would be left to his own downward spiral. I had as good as decided this in my silence. Paint for him another dark night scene and put in the centre that pendulous child's swing, in the dullness of its cherry red. If I dared to put moonlight into it, would it be the right moonlight? If I dared to put shadows on the grass, would it be the right shadow? I figured I had, at best, a few weeks before Illie either slumped into complete madness or some jolt gave him a moment of clarity. Perhaps an eventual meeting with Furkan would prove the fork in the road. Either way I would be out of there. Now that my debts were cleared back home – or as good as – the money was not important. Perhaps if Clare had filled that pause in her voice message I would have dropped the brush and palette and been out of there that moment, back to the old life with hopes of a fresh start.

I slashed at the canvas again and the blue black sparkled. I felt my arm twitch, I felt my neck lengthen. There was life in me. I thought for a moment that perhaps I could get this right and actually help the old bastard.

There was a crack, like the splitting of a tree. It was loud, violent, and echoed across the valley from the house. It grabbed me before it had even withered away, but I did not move. Then there was another, and then two more in quick succession. My mind would not admit it to me, but I knew it was gunfire. I went to the door of the tower, opened it and looked up to the house. Lights were on. Another crack. And then a few more. Without doubt they were gunshots. Scenarios went through my head, and none of them made sense, none of them were complete. I was off, running semi-cautiously along the ridge to the house, without knowing why I was heading there or what I intended to do. In my mind were the two girls. I only knew one thing for sure, and that was I was not exhibiting bravery, but it was something else – I was compelled up that ridge.

By the time I reached the house, half-crouched and with a long gait, the gunshots had ceased, and there was a terrible stillness to the whole scene. I did not run up to the side entrance, which is the way I would normally enter the house, but I went past it and tried to look in through a few of the downstairs windows. There was nothing to see. Lights were off in the dining room and the study, but I could see through cracks in the doors that hall lights were on, and then I could see a light go on that shone down the staircase. I took a few steps back and looked up to the first floor, and could see lights going on and then off again at intervals one room at a time. I was about to make my way around to the front door when a voice came from the shadows.

"What are you doing out here?"

It was Viktor, and as soon as he spoke he stepped into the light.

"I heard the gunshots, Viktor," I said.

"You heard nothing," he said. And he was holding a revolver, for goodness sake. I looked down at it by his side, and he must have seen fear in me, for his stance softened a little and he conspicuously tucked the gun into a shoulder holster inside his jacket. "You heard nothing," he repeated.

"Where are the girls?" I said. "Where are Darya and Dina?"

"They are fine," Viktor said.

And then Illie was with us, his eyes manic and bulging. He moved like a predator toward me and then past me – he too had a revolver in his hand. "We had an intruder," he said in a rapid whispered tone. I looked at Viktor, and he gave a subtle nod of the head to confirm that Illie's explanation was the case.

"And you shot at him?" I said.

Illie stopped his agitated movements and looked me in the eye. "We shot at each other," he said. "Go back to your tower."

"Is it safe?" I said.

He stopped again and gave it some thought, looked at Viktor for confirmation, and was still looking at him when he said, "It is safe." Illie's jowls shook like a bulldog, and he spoke from deep down in his cheeks. Then he went back inside the house.

Next Evgeny came out; he was also wired, but was not in the state of a man whose daughters had been harmed – he was angry, not distraught.

"Is everything okay?" I said. "Are the girls okay?"

He looked at me with an element of surprise that I had seemed so concerned, and put his hand on my shoulder and said, "Yes, everything is okay. But we will have to wait and see what happens next."

"Did you find him, Evgeny?" Viktor said.

Evgeny shook his head. "There is nothing to find in there."

I could see now through the side entrance to the kitchen and down the hallway, Darya and Dina being consoled by Illie. They were both in dressing gowns and looked shaken but strong.

Evgeny saw I was looking at them and he patted me once more on the shoulder and he said, "They are strong girls from a strong family from a strong country."

I had not even noticed Viktor had departed, but he now returned with three large searchlights. He looked at me and said, "You stay here with the girls, then." He handed one light to Evgeny and then one to Illie who came back out of the house with a marked ferocity, and the three of them were gone, in different directions, soon to be identified in the thick night only by the streams of light darting energetically from their torches.

I looked back into the house, wondering what exactly I was supposed to do if the intruder returned, and saw the girls comforting each other. I went to them.

"Are you two okay?" I said.

"We don't know how he got to us," Darya said. "We are so careful."

"Was it a burglar?" I said.

Dina shook her head. Darya looked me in the eye and there seemed to be something there, a fragment of trust that had not previously been called upon, and she said to me, "They have found us, and I now know we will have to go."

"*Who* has found you?" I said.

Darya was welling up and she said nothing, so her sister took over and said, "The men who want to kill us."

I couldn't ask anything more, as the three men returned, seemingly without any prize, and Evgeny took his daughters under his arms and walked them back upstairs to bed. I stood in the hallway with Viktor and Illie, feeling useless and confused, watching Illie bobbing up and down on the balls of his feet, the anger bubbling in his face.

"How could this happen?" he said. And I saw Viktor shoot me a look that I felt was accusatory but I could not get to the bottom of any of it there and then. Viktor said in a warm tone to Illie that he would take care of everything, and he was gone. Illie looked at me, his agitation assuaged by Viktor's words.

"I am sorry about all this, my friend," he said. He walked me into the sitting room and poured us both generous shots of bourbon. "Bourbon is better for the nerves, if yours are a little on edge."

I took the drink. Adrenaline subsiding, I was now beginning to shake.

"Evgeny and the girls will be gone by morning," Illie said. "It is the way of things. We know now that the sorry state of affairs will not end, and they will keep running."

"Who was here tonight?" I said.

Illie shrugged, drank as he stared at the thick blackness of the window glass. "It is business," he said. "A brutal business. A business I am no longer in." He looked at me and offered a pained smile. "A business I am no longer *supposed* to be in. Evgeny is not their father, he is their salvation. But they *belong* to someone else. And Evgeny... well, he has stuck his neck out for them one stretch too far this time."

"And he came to you for help?"

Illie nodded. "I provided it for a while. But I am an old man, and I can't quite do the things I used to do."

"What is it you used to do, Illie?" I said.

He chuckled in a way I had not heard before; it was hoarse and tired. "I was what you might call in any other profession, a project manager," he said. "I took care of extremely complicated projects. And I was good at it."

Evgeny entered the room. He looked at me and Illie said that it was okay to talk with me there. Evgeny looked unsure, but he went on.

"What now?" he said.

"We always knew plan B was inevitable," Illie said.

112

Fifteen

Before dawn the next day the girls were off. I slept on the balcony of the tower out in the cleansing breeze of the night air, and it was the closing of car doors that stirred me. I woke to see bags being loaded at the side entrance to the house. I quickly made my way up there, and when Evgeny saw me approaching he held up his hand and came down to meet me twenty or so yards ahead with an element of aggression.

"You do not need to be here," he said a few times.

"I want to make sure the girls are safe," I said.

"Darya and Dina are not your concern."

"Where are you taking them?"

And that was when he put his hands on my chest, without much force, but enough to know I was walking no further.

"I don't want to hurt you, painter," he said.

I could see now over his shoulder, Dina and Darya getting into the Bentley, and Dina looked over to me and gave the smallest wave with her fingers.

"I just want to be of help," I said, my face now very close to Evgeny's. He looked at me contemplatively and then said, "What could you do? You know nothing of us, of our troubles. It is best you forget all about Dina and Darya."

And he patted me on the chest where his hand had rested, gave a sad tired half-smile and turned back to the car. Viktor, who had been loading the bags, waited for Evgeny to get in, closed the door, and pushed his own heavy frame into the driver's seat. Illie, who had hugged both girls on the doorstep, waved as the car pulled off. We both watched them go, side by side.

"That was a difficult thing for us all," he said.

"Where are they going?"

He looked at me with one eye squinted into the sun. "You ask questions like that and I get suspicious."

"Suspicious of what?"

"We had been very careful."

Illie examined me, his hands on his hips, his white linen trousers and black cotton shirt billowing in the breeze that was now coming up from the valley. I was waiting for some damning phrase to come out of his mouth, for his volatility to expose itself in the cold light of day, and he licked his lips as he squinted at me, as if preparing for a kill.

"Maybe you could help," he said at last, and I did everything I could to not physically display my relief. Still I knew this might be respite – I had seen the movies and read the books where the audience is lured into a false sense of security as the villain takes the soon-to-be victim by the hand and gives them a fateful tour of the good things of life in a moment. I felt I had to be extremely careful how the next few moments went.

"I believe in you," Illie said. "And the work you are doing for me is remarkable, all things considered."

"I am glad you approve," I said nervously.

"No, no," Illie said, waving his hand. "No need to be modest. As I have told you, I know your work, but I also know *you*. With Francis – who was the first to take on this task, you understand – none had come before him – with Francis it was a matter of trying to draw blood from stone, you understand? I think Francis was a genius in his own way, but genius needs to follow its own path – otherwise it is not genius, you agree?"

I nodded.

"Indeed. So when I was asking him for these things, and

fighting with him over details – and we fought like brothers – I was in many ways trying to pull him back from his genius and make him just apply his skills. Not so easy for a man like Francis. And it took much time for him to get at what I was needing him to get at. In the end he found my voice, but it took time. With you, it took one evening. You have skills but no genius. Now, no, no, do not take offence at this. Genius is important to human faith but it is not *all-important*. Imagine where the human race would be if we were all of us geniuses. Who would make the wheels turn? That is not the job of the genius. No. We need great men like yourself. Great artists, to make sure things get done and the world is explained."

"And dreams," I said, contentiously.

Illie tossed this over in his head for a moment.

"You think you are helping me *interpret* my dreams? You think that is what Francis was doing?"

"I'm not sure what you want my work to do, Illie," I said, exasperation and fatigue easily overcoming my nervousness.

"I do not need this dream *interpreted*. I need it *painted*. There is something in it, and I need to focus."

He had seemed to shrink before me, seemed to age, as if he was now some ancient creature afraid of the light.

"Somebody said to me you are looking for buried treasure."

He looked up at me and that squint returned, but it was not a look of shock. Something was coming over him.

"Who said this?" he said.

"A local," I said. "An islander. I doubt you know him."

"But he knows me, it seems."

I felt like I'd been hit with a bat.

"So it's money. This is all about money."

Illie shook his head sadly.

"No," he said slowly. "Not money. I am looking for my son."

His tone belied the gravitas of what he had just said, and I

115

wondered if Francis had ever gotten this far with him. My mind immediately returned to the dangers of this place.

"Illie," I said, and I placed my hand on his forearm, "who was here last night?"

He curled his bottom lip and bobbed his head up and down, looking to the ground. "A bad man. Come to kill Evgeny, and the girls if he can get to them. He won't get to them now."

"Where have they gone?"

"Come and paint for me," he said, in a tone that did not suggest a change of subject, but he gestured with his head over to the tower and began to walk there.

As we walked he said, "They have gone to a secret place, much more secret than here; a place where even if you knew it existed you would not follow them."

"Where?"

"A ghost city."

"They have gone to Famagusta?"

He looked at me. "You have heard of it?"

"It's been explained to me."

He curled his lip again and bobbed his head. "Interesting choice of words."

"What?"

"That you have it *explained to you*. And who explained it? Your waitress?"

I suddenly felt as if things were falling away from me, as if I had been sure I was existing on the edges of a drama, when in fact all along it had been happening all around me.

"Viktor told you about Lou?" I asked calmly. We were almost at the door of the tower by this point.

"Paint for me," Illie said, and lifted his arm out to the doorway.

He ushered me inside the tower and spoke whilst remaining outside. "I know you are a friend to me," he said. "And after what happened last night there was a great deal to think about. But

116

now I have done my thinking. You may be able to help with Famagusta. Paint for now, and we will talk more tomorrow."

He closed the door on me, and the silence of the room combined with the pulsing heat of the place pressed on me hard. I felt too nauseous to even look at the paint and its sweet smell was too strong. I wanted to call Clare, but what was there to say? It was clear to me that our problems were now separate ones; just as they had converged when we had, now they diverged as we came to terms with the splitting of our single self. That loneliness was the harshest winter of all the weather of our separation. The realisation I would have to be miserable in silence, on my own.

And this was not simply misery, it was an inability to force defiance into the real space before me. Helplessness. It was striking how quickly you can forget how powerful a feeling helplessness is. So I painted. I tore at that canvas as if I was possessed, I swung at it and gritted my teeth and hit at it, and fell exhausted back into the armchair. Illie believed that in this scene somewhere was the location of his son. Perhaps I had hit a stride – perhaps Illie had got me into the state he wanted me in – for this painting was indistinguishable from the others.

Sixteen

There were police at Lou's place. They had found a body up near the coves and they were looking for ways to identify it. I said to the policeman who seemed to carry himself with more authority than the others that Lou worked at The Castle and that they must have had some employment records there of some sort that would help.

"We have spoken to the manager here," he said, ushering me a little down the corridor away from Lou's room. "There is no record of Miss Louise Brighthead working in Cyprus."

"What are you talking about?"

"Relax," said the policeman. "You thought she worked at The Castle?"

"That's where I met her, she was waiting tables."

He nodded and made a note in his flip-top pad.

"So perhaps she got a job there the last few days," he said.

"No, that isn't it," I said. "She has been working there for six months. At least six months."

The officer looked at me, as if to say that this chapter is done with. And then a thought occurred to him.

"You knew her well?" he said.

I shook my head. "No, not well. We met a few days ago."

"But you could identify her."

My heart sank, and the saliva in my mouth became a metallic liquid. "I'm not your man for that," I said.

"You knew her in *that* way?" the policeman said.

My head was heavy, foggy, and I was trying to glimpse over

his shoulder through the door to Lou's room where other officers were going through her things. "*That* way? You mean, was I sleeping with her?"

"Sleeping, yes." He smiled sarcastically.

"We went out for the day. She gave me a tour of the island. No funny business."

He wrote, again with an edge of sarcasm, into his pad. "*No funny business*."

"Can I ask what happened?" I said.

"Difficult to say. It is potentially dangerous up around those coves. The body was pretty badly beaten up on the rocks."

"You think she fell?"

He nodded, as if to say that she had most likely come off the cliffs but how or why was anybody's guess.

He took my details, and I gave him the name of the hotel I had stayed at in Protaras when I first arrived for Francis's funeral. I did not want to give him Illie's name, and I didn't know the address. I had forgotten that I did not know the address.

I walked slowly back to the car parked on the upper main street. I had known Lou just a few days, and there was no confirmation the body was in fact her, but I felt oppressively sad on that short walk; it was heavier than the heat, and pushed me down as if I moved through polluted water. It was a sadness more profound than if she had just been a passing acquaintance, as I had tried to portray her to the policeman. A more profound sadness than even if I had simply warmed to her, wanted to get her into bed. I hadn't realised that I had fallen for her a little bit. Enough to hit me hard.

I was yards from the car – it all happened quick – when clarity came to me like the jab of a blade through the heat. Lou had been killed and I knew why. *They* had thought it was her. They had muddled through their numbskull reasoning and come up with *her* name. Viktor had asked me about Lou, and I had lied to him.

Illie had asked me about her and I had lied to him. They had seen through these lies and seen some insane picture. They were focussing on her as the source of the night-time attack. Who else knew the girls were at the house? I had let it slip. They had got it wrong. So wrong. Illie had killed Lou.

I drove quickly back to Illie's along the razor-edge tarmac of the highways, expecting my rage to subside, for reason to take over, but the opposite happened. It was fury that did the driving, and blind rage that got me out of the car and charging to the house, through the front door, into each room in turn, calling Illie's name, barging past furniture and ornaments, and then in the kitchen he was there and as he turned to me I grabbed him by the shirt and pushed him up against the wall. This old man now had the chance to show me what he was made of, and his eyes were wide and red – and was that the edge of a grin on his mouth? I slammed him again up against the wall and I said to him, "You killed her, you fuck, and you were wrong – you were wrong about her." I had meant to say so much and to beat his grinning face into the wall, but my slams became weaker, and the adrenaline seeped out of me like from an hourglass. I was beginning to ramble incoherently about Lou and murder, and this was when Illie rose up, the huge dome of his shoulders breaking my grip, and then a blow to my midriff the likes of which I had never felt before – it took the wind right out of my body as if it was my soul escaping – I don't know if it was from his fists or forearms or from his knee, but it crumpled me, and he caught me before I fell to the floor. Without even knowing he was there, I was in Viktor's arms, and he moved me like a rag doll to the kitchen door and flung me out into the dirt. I coughed into the ground for a second, part of me bracing for the next blow that might well have been the fatal one. I was numb, and my thoughts were all over the place – I remember thinking if this is life flashing before the eyes then my life had been a real mess.

But no second blow came. I got to my knees – I had landed with my arse to the door I had been flung from – and I turned, holding my gut, and faced the house. Illie and Viktor stood on the step looking down at me.

"The painter turned out to be brave," Viktor said.

"And dumb," Illie said

"And predictable," said Viktor.

"And full of surprises," said Illie.

"Are you going to kill me?" I said.

They looked at each other. "No," Illie said. "You see, I have a problem, and that is that I have already decided that you are my friend. Friends fall out, sure. But real friends share a bond."

Even at this low ebb I was having none of it.

"You killed Lou," I said.

"Fuck. Do you *want* me to kill you? Is that it?" Illie said. "Goading me. Where do you think that is going to get you?" He came down the step and took a few paces toward me. "You're talking about the waitress?" He looked back at Viktor who nodded confirmation. "I didn't kill her."

"Viktor," I said, tossing a glance at Illie's henchman.

Illie looked back at him and then at me. "No." He shook his head as one might to a child. "Viktor went to speak with her. I needed to know who she worked for."

"She worked at The Castle, Illie. She was just a fucking waitress," I said.

"Ah, my dear painter friend. No. She was no waitress. She was working for someone who was looking for Evgeny and the girls. And she's not the only one on the island. We have heard rumours from my people back in Russia that they had been looking here. Whispers always sprout up over time. The kind of people who were looking… well, they live on whispers like that, like hyenas live on discarded bones. So I was waiting for people like your waitress to show themselves. You told her we were here. And then

121

we get a night-time visit. So Viktor had to go and speak with her. But he didn't kill her."

"None of this makes any sense," I said.

"I couldn't find her," Viktor said stepping forward. "Likely she was already dead. Killed by whoever she passed the information onto."

I shuffled my legs under me and sat my behind down in the dirt. There was silence then for a while, just the buzzing of the midday heat. They were not going to kill me, and when my heart levelled, and the sadness of the idea of Lou's murder had returned, I felt myself start to weep into my cuffs. Illie was walking away back into the house and I heard him say to Viktor, "We will prepare some dinner. No painting today."

Seventeen

Illie was stood over me when I awoke in the armchair.

"I told you no painting," he said in an avuncular tone.

I rubbed my eyes and straightened myself up, and looked around the room. My head had a sharp pain going through the middle, the transfiguration of what had been in the now empty brandy bottle I spotted on the desk. An unfinished canvas was sitting on the easel, but I could see two more that had been started leaning next to it on the floor. I could not remember much of the previous night. I recalled what had happened in the house, and my comeuppance outside the kitchen, but nothing after it. I think there was some kind of breakdown involved and, obviously, booze. I had sobbed, alone, in the tower. I thought hard while trying not to look like I was thinking about anything as Illie examined the work.

"But this is good," he said eventually.

"You think I have it?" I said, kneading my forehead with my knuckles.

"I think today you will paint more," Illie said. "Keep up momentum, yes?"

He took the unfinished work from the easel and then began to gather the others.

"You are approaching the right feel for the red of the centre," he said. I scratched my head. I had been concentrating so hard on devising a formula and a mix for the grey blue silver of the night that I had been just sloshing up the child's swing. I would get to that later, I had thought.

123

Illie was back at the door now, the canvases under his arm. "Paint," he said, and he was gone.

Now alone, I could adjust myself and allow a groan that expressed all the creaks of my dehydrated state. I poured a tumbler of water from the sink and dropped in some dissolving tablets, watching them fizz and break apart. What was to be done? Lou's name careered around inside my head like a funeral chant. There was no time for this anymore, I thought. I necked the milky water, and cracked my neck, and went to the door. It took a moment to see where Illie had gone – I thought at first he must have sprinted up to the house, but then I came out a little and looked across the flats, then I came out a little further and looked down to see if he had gone down to the pool, and then over the opposite side of the ridge to see down to the woodland. And I just caught him, a small shadowed figure, entering the wood by the east side. I waited for him to be gone and then I went down after him.

The track was not finished, perhaps purposely difficult to navigate, steep and covered in shale. I was very careful not to kick rocks down the incline and alert him to my movements. I came to the edge of the wood and then realised that the trees were actually quite spare, but that their tops were fulsome and almost totally blocked out the sun and heat. It was extremely dingy in there. I know nothing of trees, but they were pale-trunked with heavy charcoal dapples across them, and they were not all that tall – maybe only two or three times the height of a man. I went in.

I was only a few steps into the wood when I saw the first canvas nailed to one of those trees. It was not one of mine, and didn't look like one of mine, although the content was the same – the dark background drawing the eye in to a red child's swing just off centre left. I knew immediately this was the work of Francis Benthem. Then there was another one on the tree just to the right of it. This was most certainly *not* the work of Francis. It was extremely amateurish. If Illie had been telling the truth when he told me Francis was his first artist, then I had to assume that this was an early attempt of Illie's to create his own depiction of this dream. And then I saw another canvas. And then another. All nailed to trunks of different trees. The dark background and the red child's swing just off to the left of centre. I could not see Illie anywhere, or see any trace of him, and so I walked deeper into the wood, and as I did so the canvases multiplied, all with the same image and composition, and soon the trunks bore more than one canvas and soon there were trees that held two canvases, three canvases, and everywhere I turned was the polka dot red of the child's swing pricking out of the blue silver grey background. And now that background of the canvases was beginning to draw into it the natural light of the wood, and everything was beginning to mesh and my eyes were growing blurry. This was when I heard Illie's voice.

"In all his time in that tower, Francis never once followed me down here," he said. He was behind me, leaning against a tree. "Foolish of me not to take this into account when the two of you have turned out to be so different in so many ways."

"Francis never wanted to know what you were doing?"

"Oh, I'm sure he did frequently wonder. But he never followed me down here. We had a kind of unwritten understanding. Unspoken. He would paint and I would take them. I suppose he must have wondered if one day it would all stop. He would paint the right painting and I would tell him to leave. I suppose he felt the less he knew, the less there was a chance of him getting it right. I see that now."

Illie took a few steps and gestured for me to follow him. He took me to a small clearing, where the canvases seemed at their most dense, and he took me to a chair.

"I sit here," he said. "And I try to pick apart the dream. The dream, you see, is the key to finding my son."

"Tell me about your son, Illie."

125

"The only thing I have left on this sorry Earth."

"I didn't know you had a son."

"Nobody does. Nobody except for Tara."

In the dimness of the shaded wood, some things began to shift into place.

"Tara knows?"

"I was working for a Russian hotelier who had, shall we say, some difficult competitors in Famagusta. It was nineteen seventy-three. I was sent over to run the *project*." He moved his hands at this word, as if feeling the circumference of a globe in mid-air. "While there I met Tara. She was waiting tables. We began an affair. You will ask me if it was love." He curled his bottom lip. "These are complicated words. Tara seems to have a more intense recollection that might have had something to do with some kind of love. I wanted her to get rid of the baby. My line of work was not the line of work that encouraged a positive view of the world and its inhabitants. I had no intention of bringing a child into the world." He took a long pause. I thought he might be choking back tears. "But I could see a life with Tara. Maybe things could be different. Then the invasion happened. She had the baby on its eve – can you believe that? July nineteenth. If there is a God, he is one for signs, I would say. That was *quite* the sign. Well, *I* saw it as a sign – God or no God – and I took Tara from the hospital." He paused again, something caught in his throat. "I left the baby boy. I figured the Turks could have him, bring him up. Show him the world. You look at me as if I am making this up. I was a different man. A hard man. Shrewd. Not superstitious. Not sentimental. I did not know this little lump of flesh and bone. All I knew was that I needed Tara. I did not need anything else."

"You left the baby in the hospital?"

"I did."

"And you have no idea if he survived."

Illie took to the chair. He looked exhausted all of a sudden.

126

"Tara could not forgive me. I returned to Russia without her. I did not think of Cyprus again until my wife died and the dreams began."

"What do you hope all this is going to do?" I said.

"It is going to show me where my son is," he said. "I know the answer is in here somewhere." He tapped his temple with his forefinger, but he also meant that the answer was in this wood. He was creating an internal world.

I looked around at the canvases hanging from the trees – I now also had a strong sense that Francis was truly in on this, even if he had never asked as many questions as me. I still believed that Illie was mad, but now I wondered if he thought it too – that he could find the child he so callously abandoned by mapping out his dream images in this dark wood. Nobody could fail to see this for what it was – a desperate act by a man terrified he had led his life, soon to pass, immorally.

"Is Tara aware of all this?" I said gesturing at the paintings.

"I have tried to stay away from her," he said. "I did not wish to drag things up for her. But I feel Furkan will have answers."

"So why not just go up to Furkan and ask him? Why are you bothered now about Tara's feelings?"

"Furkan will not speak to me unless Tara tells him to."

"And what do you hope to get from him?"

Illie kicked his toe into the dirt and thought for a moment. "Everybody knows the Golden Orphans know more than they let on. They have contact with those who were left behind. And they know more things about the secrets of this island than anybody will dare admit. Why do you think they are regarded here the way they are?" He leaned forward in the chair and spoke in a low voice. "I know my son is alive somewhere on this island. And I *know* I can find him."

I looked around once more and wondered just how this could possibly end. "So you sit here?" I said.

"The answer is in here somewhere," he said. "It just has to be done right. Every night I walk in my sleep through this island, through its secrets, and I see my son, and I speak to him, and I make amends, and we are good with each other. And every morning I awake and all I can see is this red swing in this dark night."

"Illie," I said, "I will paint for you as long as you need me to paint for you. But I need to know who killed Lou."

He looked up at me, a glaze to his eyes, and he said, "Why?"

I was trying to find an answer, trying to summon something that made sense, but faintly we were both alerted to a voice in the distance. It was Evgeny calling Illie's name.

Illie looked up to me, his eyes now wide and his face old and tired. "Go see him for me, will you? I need to be here today."

Eighteen

Evgeny was calling into the air – it looked as though he had already searched the house for Illie, and the tower, and was heading back along the ridge. I caught up with him and told him Illie was in the wood and he didn't want to be disturbed.

"Then you will have to come," he said. He said it with urgency, without much contemplation of who I was or what had gone before. "We have found the tunnel, but we need supplies," he said, walking quickly back to the house. "We need to follow my girls with supplies."

Back in the house Viktor was already filling cardboard boxes with anything he could find in the kitchen cupboards. Evgeny turned to me. "Fill these boxes with food. Anything that would be good for a camping trip, for instance," he said. "I am going to get more blankets."

"You have taken the girls to the neutral zone?"

He stopped and glared at me. "Are you going to help or not?"

I said nothing and as he went off out of the kitchen I could hear him grumbling something about too many questions.

We packed the car with several cardboard boxes of tinned and packet food, and Evgeny filled the boot with blankets and sleeping bags. As Viktor drove with calmness in speed, Evgeny only spoke to begrudgingly answer my sparse questions.

"Famagusta is different to what we thought," he said without looking at me. "Illie said it was a safe place. A ghost town. But the girls will need to be taken care of while they hide there."

After some time on the road we spun off track and Viktor

129

drove with great haste and concentration across a scrub field. After a while we could see a wall emerge from amidst the foliage of an orangery, and at first I thought little of it, until we came closer and the wall grew higher and higher and Evgeny pointed out that we were in fact approaching the tunnel entrance. Past the orangery was a disused chapel, overgrown with broken grey trees reaching their broken grey branches protectively over the stonework. It would not have been visible from the road, now quite a way back, sunk into the browns and charcoals of the countryside. I peered as far as I could see beyond the wall, and there was no sign of any town, abandoned or otherwise. Viktor pulled up with a snarl of the tyres into the gravel of the weedy chapel forecourt, and was out of the car seemingly before he had even stalled the engine. He and Evgeny began unloading the boot.

"The tunnel is through here," Evgeny said carrying boxes past him. I lifted more and followed him.

The chapel was in disrepair in every quarter: the windows smashed, the pews knocked over like dominoes, the altar smashed and Christ on the Cross fallen and tilted up against the wall. The light slipped in through broken slats in the window shades.

"Here," Evgeny called from near what once must have been the vestry. He pushed back a heavy curtain revealing a door. Opening it, he lifted his boxes once again and disappeared down steps into darkness. I looked at Viktor, aiming for some support in my apprehension at the prospect of following Evgeny into the cellar, but of course there was nothing forthcoming. Viktor looked at me dead on, impassive, a man who only knew how to commit his body to motion. I might have imagined deep thought processes behind those heavy dark eyes of his, but in truth there was most likely nothing, no warmth toward me as I sometimes might have hoped; no sympathy, no humour. I wanted to slap him across the back and ask him what he thought of all this, but it was unlikely he thought anything. He just went about his work, no task any more unusual than the next.

In the cellar a lamp was already lit, and the blockage to the tunnel had already been removed from the entrance. Evgeny was readjusting his burden, and he looked at me and said, "How is your stamina, painter?" I nodded gingerly, but I knew it was not with confidence, and he motioned with a dip of his head for me to follow him into the tunnel.

It was dark, but it was not long, and took just a few minutes to reach the fresh air. Viktor had followed behind me, and I could hear the big guy breathing heavily at the mid point, and then more lightly. We came out into a small barn-of-sorts, and Evgeny led us out into more orangery – the partition had split some farmer's land right down the middle.

"They just cut this land in two," I said, using my observation as an excuse to catch my breath.

"Come," Evgeny said. "We don't have time. Every moment we are away the girls are in danger."

We lifted our boxes, and Evgeny his blankets too, and marched through the trees. We were just a few steps when Viktor grabbed Evgeny by the forearm. "We are followed," he said in a hushed voice looking back in the direction from which we had come. Evgeny cursed in Russian and we moved off to the side behind some trees and peered back toward the barn. Evgeny cursed a few more times.

"We cannot lead him right to the girls," he said.

Viktor carefully put down his boxes. "There was always this risk going back to the house," he said, and took a revolver from his concealed shoulder holster.

I was paralysed behind my tree, but still managed to speak. "Who the fuck is following us?"

"The man from the other night," Evgeny whispered.

131

The killer, I thought. The *hired* killer. I looked at Evgeny and at Viktor and felt no safer. Evgeny had now also armed himself.

"There," Viktor whispered and pointed his gun. I saw nothing at first, but when he said it a second time, I saw some movement in the far distance shimmering quickly from left to right against the backdrop of the wall. Viktor fired his gun. Evgeny cursed again in Russian. "There are guards here," he said. Viktor peered out, looking to see where he had hit. A voice called out. We all looked at each other. "Don't shoot." It was a female voice. I knew immediately that I recognised it but my brain wouldn't engage.

"Who the fuck?" Evgeny said, and he stepped out from behind the tree, his gun raised. "Who is that?" he called. There was a reply, and I stepped out too because now I knew it was Lou.

And there she was, with her hands raised, stepping out, untouched by Viktor's bullet, and very much alive. I gasped – I heard myself do it – and it alerted Evgeny and Viktor to the fact that I recognised our tail.

"This is Lou," I said.

"The waitress who gave us up?" said Evgeny.

"Told you I didn't kill her," said Viktor looking at me with a shrug.

Evgeny had not lowered his gun, and so Lou stayed rooted to her spot.

"What are you doing here?" he said. "The police thought you were dead. *We* thought you were dead."

It was only now I could see how shaken she was, and not just as a result of being shot at – it was something deeper than that.

"I need to hide," she said. "I followed you because I knew you were looking for the tunnel. Somebody's trying to kill me."

I walked to her, much to the annoyance of Evgeny. She looked exhausted, she was dirty and sunburned and on touching her hands in a gesture of comfort I felt them trembling.

"*Who* is trying to kill you?" I said. I walked her slowly to the other two.

"Stelly." She trembled as she said the name. "He mistook some other girl for me, I think. He thinks he killed me. I stayed away from my place so he would go on thinking that."

"Why Stelly?"

"He is a bounty hunter," Viktor interjected. "A Cypriot bum doing somebody else's dirty work."

"The ones who you are running from?" I said to Evgeny. He nodded morosely. "Why didn't you kill him before now?"

Evgeny cursed and looked to the sky. "You think you know everything about our world now, is that it? We just go around slaughtering people we think we do not like?"

That brought a silence to the group.

"I don't know anything about anything," Lou said eventually. "I just know he hit me for this information. He said he was going to do terrible things to me. I managed to escape and I ran down into Protaras and he came after me and in the end he must have caught up to someone he thought was me."

She began to weep, and it seemed like the first real unloading since she went missing. I held her.

"Let me come with you," she said. "Stelly is looking for me."

"And he is looking for us now too," Evgeny said. "Because of you." The tone changed, and Evgeny stepped forward to us both with a look of fire in his eyes. "We cannot take you with us when you put us in danger. I should kill you."

"Dammit, Evgeny." I felt anger come up through me – not just anger, a frustration and sadness – and it took me aback just as much as it did everybody else. "She did not give you up lightly. It is that fucking cockroach Stelly who is to blame and only him." Evgeny seemed to take a step back, but I was not done, it seemed. "In fact, it is not only him, is it? This whole fucking mess is because of who you people are. The only people who aren't to

133

blame are Darya and Dina. And God knows Lou hasn't done anything wrong. You may have rescued them, but what did you pull them out from? Your own fucking world, Evgeny. So don't get all holier-than-thou with us. Lou is coming with us because she needs our help. And she needs that help because your fucked up world, and Viktor's fucked up world, and Illie's fucked up world, just ruins lives. And it might have ruined hers, and it might still yet ruin mine. So she's coming with us."

He thought about it, but he gave in. And the four of us set off for Famagusta with our boxes of supplies through the dry heat of the orangery.

Nineteen

Famagusta rose from the scrub like a giant carcass, the whitewashed bones of abandoned buildings rutting up into the skyline, each crawled over with linden and the charcoal-grey branches of barren poplars. The breeze that had followed us whistled hollow through the first streets we tentatively walked down. We walked slowly, stepping carefully – we were just specks in a silent empty thoroughfare, suspicious that we were being watched, ripe for an ambush, and perhaps apprehensive that we were stepping into a fiction. When it had been described as a ghost town none of us had suspected such a pallid lifeless scene: abandoned storefronts, dirt-smudged windows glistening in the sunlight, pavements overrun with weeds, sandstorm dust piles in corners smoothly mounding up to a point. And again the silence. It was otherworldly. It was not quiet, for we could hear the sparse chatter of birds, the breeze rustling through the wild foliage, but between these movements was a deep and dank silence, as if it hung heavy with moisture, the kind of silence I imagined that is only possible where there is no-one to hear it.

By now I had the food boxes up on my shoulder; my shirt was soaked through, rivulets of sweat ran down my spine, and the dust had kicked up around my knees. Lou was exhausted. Her arms hung and her eyes strained out from two dark circles. On the walk each of us had taken it in turns to question her further on what had gone on that night she had been attacked, and what had happened since. Each of us had, without combined strategy, taken different roles. Evgeny had been aggressive, dismissive of

135

her answers, and had made his case to both Viktor and myself for leaving her behind before we reached Famagusta. Viktor had been cold and pragmatic about the whole affair and eventually admitted that Stelly would have to be eliminated, and that Lou was an asset in this ambition, not a handicap. But I had only had my sympathy. Inside her somewhere I could see her resilience flicker like a pilot light every time one of the others held back to sling a question at her. "Who is this dead woman?" "Where can we find Stelly?" "How long have you known about Prostakov and the girls?" Each time she rose higher to answer. And with each question I found myself standing closer by her.

"Keep moving," Evgeny barked at us straggling behind him. "The Turks will still be looking for the source of Viktor's gunshot earlier. Keep your wits about you."

The street widened and the buildings rose higher. This was the central part of Famagusta. Old hotel signs hung rusted and faded outside open-mouthed foyers, a truck sat like a boulder at the side of the road, the carriage labelled with some long out-fashioned cigarette logo flashed in a lively ribbon across the tarp.

"Where are the girls?" said Viktor.

"I walked them down here to a hotel, and they were told to wait for me," Evgeny replied.

The weight of the food boxes had now finally cramped up my arms and I let them down as gently as I could onto the floor. "I need to stop," I said. "Just for a moment or two. I cannot feel my arms."

Evgeny grumbled something Russian, but Lou mouthed a thank you at me, and Viktor began to circle where we stopped, looking up at every window in every hotel and office block. He too felt there were eyes upon us.

"I can see now how the stories come about," Lou said.

"What stories?" Evgeny said irritably.

"Of the people who would hide out here," she said. "All these windows feel like eyes watching us."

Evgeny sniggered.

"That tunnel has always been there. Long before 'seventy-four," he said without looking at her.

Viktor looked Evgeny up and down.

"I am told this is the case," Evgeny said. "It was not built by criminals. It was built by soldiers during the war."

"What do you know about the people who live here now?" I said.

Evgeny laughed.

"Nobody *lives* in here," he said. "That is all a myth."

Viktor did not look so sure and Evgeny caught this.

"You think there are bandits here?" Evgeny all but squared up to Viktor.

"I wouldn't be so sure as you are of a place I had never been to," Viktor said.

There was a noise, a rumble in the distance, and we all looked down the main street from the direction we had come. Nobody said anything, but we knew it was the distant sound of a military jeep, and we hurriedly picked up our boxes and made haste toward the hotel where Evgeny had left the girls.

The jeep was getting louder as Evgeny led us down a side alley and then into the tradesman's entrance of a building. By the time we had all made it in, and through to an inner room, I was ready to collapse in the thick stale air that buzzed with heavy heat and a swirl of acrid smells. Evgeny ushered us further, and as we reached the first floor we could see the jeep with two armed guards go by the hotel and carry on down the road toward the beach.

"No more guns," Evgeny said as we watched them pass.

The hotel interior, although dilapidated, was eerily awake with the sense of business. Tables remained laid, rugs remained down, beds were made. Clear the dust and it could have opened up the next day for customers.

Dina and Darya were in one of the hotel suites, Dina sitting peeking out from behind the heavy curtains to the street, and Darya pacing in the dim light. They were happy to see us, but this changed quickly to apprehension.

"Who is this?" Darya said.

"This is Lou," I said.

Viktor seemed to sense the danger implicit in the question and moved to the window with his gun drawn.

"Lou is a friend who has gotten caught up in all this," I tried to explain.

Darya looked her up and down disapprovingly.

"Someone is watching us," Dina said, and her sister shot her a look. "We know the stories."

Dina got up from her seat and stood by Viktor at the window, pointing between the crack in the curtains. Evgeny joined them and looked between the two across the street to the buildings opposite. "I was keeping lookout for you, in case you missed us, and I saw someone across the street, in that window, and he was looking straight back at me."

"What did the man look like?" Evgeny said.

Dina had nothing else. She saw the outline of a figure, the sparkled reflection from a window as the figure moved. And this was exactly the kind of haunted netherworld where light would play tricks. I tried to calm the situation a little by saying, "Why don't we go through these boxes and try and get you girls settled in." As I said it I looked at Lou for support, but everyone else seemed to take it as something else.

"She can't stay here," Darya said. "We don't know her."

"But where is she supposed to go?" I said.

Lou was tugging at my elbow. "Leave it," she said.

"We only let her come this far in the hope she might be useful to us," Evgeny said.

I noticed then that his pistol was drawn once again, and had

138

probably been so for some time. His eyes were burning at the edges and his skin was turning a freckled grey. He had taken something.

"Let's just all relax before we start making decisions on things like this," I said. I opened the one box as a gesture and began slowly unloading the tins.

"Not here," Evgeny said.

"What's wrong with here?" I asked.

Darya was pacing again, and Viktor stepped away from the window – he also had his revolver in his hand. And then Dina, still peering out from the gap in the curtains said, "Who is that man?"

The room stopped, everyone still for a moment, then Evgeny, with his amphetamine edginess, went quickly to the window and pushed Dina to one side. He turned back to the room, and to me he said, "Get the girls away from here. He saw me. Get them away. Up."

"Who is it?" I said.

Evgeny did not answer, but he pushed the girls toward me. Viktor looked out of the window, and I went past Evgeny and looked out too, and just caught a glimpse of the unmistakable shape of Stelly coming toward the main entrance of the hotel. "How did he find us?" I said.

Evgeny had his own theories, and as I turned he had Lou by the throat up against the wall and was spitting some Russian into her face. Dina and Darya began to make noises that belied their nerves. Viktor did not move from the window, and it was I, without much thought, who leapt toward Evgeny and wrapped my arms around his shoulders from behind and pulled and pulled, and he came loose of Lou who collapsed to the floor gasping for breath, and we both went tumbling back over the bed and landed on opposite sides. We got to our knees quickly. Evgeny felt around his body for his gun – he had dropped it, and

I know that if he had landed with it in his hand he would have shot me immediately. He saw it on the floor, was about to lunge, but now Viktor stepped up, put his shin across Evgeny's path and said simply, "We do not have time for this. The waitress has drawn him out. We will deal with her later. Get the girls to the roof."

As I led Dina, Darya and Lou down the corridor I spoke some thoughts out loud: "Why do Evgeny and Viktor seem so frightened of Stelly? He is just one small man." And Darya answered, in a stern calm voice that I had not heard from her before, "These people we run from are not to be taken lightly, and neither are the people they hire to work for them."

We moved quickly, although Lou lagged slightly; she panted and grimaced and was all but bent double with exhaustion. Just as I was about to lift her, Dina took her by the arm, although Darya tutted and urged her sister to hurry along. But Lou, who smiled at Dina and thanked her, pulled her arm back and said that she needed to go back to the room we had just left.

"Where are you going?" I said. "We need to get on the roof."

But she pulled away. "I left something," she said. "I need to tell Evgeny something. He needs to know something."

She straightened and walked back down the corridor, and a curious thing came to me then: she had said Evgeny's name, and it sounded clear and tireless in her mouth, as if it lifted her, as if it had been pronounced by those lips a thousand times. As my ears tried to understand the subtle perfection of her voice, I also then became sure that none of us had spoken our names at any point during the walk from the tunnel to the hotel.

I stood there with these thoughts and everything turned calm.

I called to her as she walked away, but then one of the girls shrieked and I turned and could see the unmistakable silhouette of Stelly right down the far end of the corridor; his taut diminutive shape in that ugly little dance he did on the balls of his toes, his

140

head made square by the frayed-brim cap he was never without. He looked as if he was waiting for us. We all stood still for a moment. I then saw we were just a few steps from the emergency staircase and I quickly pushed the girls through the door and I told them to go up – "Get up to the roof and jam the door shut behind you when you get there" – and no sooner had I said it than the dense silver echo of gunshots began to clack behind us. I pushed the girls with one arm as I dived to crouch inside the doorway, and they both ran up the staircase. I turned and leaned on the frame to sneak one eye. Another gunshot and then several more. They overlapped and I lost count, and then I could see Stelly, coming slowly down the corridor with no gun so far as I could make out – but of course I had no weapon either, and the closer Stelly's silhouette advanced down toward my position the more I could feel a hopeless situation emerging. More gunshots. This all happened in just a few seconds, three bursts of gunfire from several guns, and now I could tell the shots were coming from the other end of the corridor – and in the distance somewhere outside of the hotel was the hurried growl of jeep engines coming through the concave echoes of the deserted streets.

Another gunshot, but this time down the corridor and Stelly dived for cover – no, it was not a dive, but a smooth movement to the side and he bent carefully into a doorway. He was just a few yards from my position now, and I peeked out and he saw me and our eyes locked and, by god, if he didn't grin that lipless grin of his at me.

It was what I needed, this jolt of electricity from this repugnant humanoid, and I darted into the corridor and down toward the room, but I was no more than half way when Lou emerged from it, stumbled from it, although she straightened quickly and it was clear she was not hurt, and that she was holding a gun. In the movement and from the mist of adrenaline, my first thought was that it was not Evgeny or Viktor's gun.

"Where are the others?" I said, but Lou lifted her pistol and fired several times – I hit the floor quicker than my weight would force me down, but she continued to fire, not at me, but past me, the bullets splintering the doorframe Stelly was hiding behind. I looked over my shoulder from the ground to see Stelly rush in his bare feet across the corridor and attempt to clatter through the emergency staircase door, but as he did so Lou continued to shoot and in the last yard she hit him – in the side or the arm or the head, it was impossible to tell at that pace – but blood spilled, it puffed into the air, and he went through the door headfirst with legs buckling, like a battering ram.

And then there was silence and Lou was standing over me.

She was breathing heavily and did not take her eyes off the doorway.

"What the fuck is going on?" I managed to say, but I don't know how audible I was. She stepped forward slowly with the revolver pointed to where Stelly had crashed. The silence hissed, and somewhere outside of the hotel more than one jeep screeched to a halt in the street. It seemed imperative to move and I got to my feet, facing the room where Evgeny and Viktor still were. I watched Lou, who seemed to have cast off her exhaustion miraculously and now handled the gun with unnerving confidence – she reached the doorway and her shoulders tensed. "What is it?" I called. But she didn't acknowledge me, and instead, with gun still raised, she entered the stairwell.

I quickly went for the room but made it no further than the doorway. The easiest way to describe it would be to say it was all shot up. The curtain rails were splintered and down, the feathers from the bed were scattered all around and hung lightly in the air, the mirror on the wall was shattered. In the middle of the detritus lay both Evgeny and Viktor, on their backs, bloodied and still, riddled with the dark puncture holes of Lou's revolver.

She had played me. Tricked me from the beginning. As I tried to catch my breath in that doorway, transfixed for a moment by the awful scene, it all came to me what a fool I had been. This dream world I had entered, this insanity, lured by Francis Benthem into a place I could not see was Hell; it had devoured him, and it was about to spit me out. I felt the surge come up behind me. *Spit me out. Spit me out.* I could feel the opportunity for escape. It was a crack in the glass, a moment in the motion that held me. I could run. *I could run.*

And then clarity. Lou would not be done with killing Stelly – she was welcome to *him* – but she was going after Dina and Darya. It was she, also, I could see now, who had murdered the woman and put the body in her own place. She had played me, and she had used Stelly as a demon to draw our suspicions and fears. This all spread through my mind, as if I was laying the facts out in order on a desk, piece by piece. And then the sound of boots. Turkish guards were in the building and heading up the stairs. With hands shaking and a mind that was sure it would regret the decision, I picked up Viktor's pistol from beside his body and ran to the emergency stairwell. There was blood on the stairs – Stelly's – and I followed it.

As I headed up I could hear the boots behind me in the corridor below and the voices of orders barked in Turkish. Up and up further still; the door to the roof was closed and there was no sign of anyone before it. My heart thundered in my chest, made my chest plate shake like an old tin tray, but I was moving ahead of myself now and with one push I went out onto the roof. A part of me – perhaps a part of my soul I had never encountered before – expected me to die the moment I stepped out into the light. But there was no gunfire. I was not shot. The scene on the rooftop was quite something else.

Darya and Dina were quite safe, I could see straight away, both standing near the wall of a utility block. As soon as I spotted them I was overcome with the heat. It boomed. I spun and looked for Lou. She was sitting, her back against the wall at the edge of the roof, and Stelly was next to her, also sitting. That was when my eyes adjusted to the brightness and I saw the whole scene as one, and that we were now all under the command of five others, all of them armed, some kind of militia.

Everyone seemed remarkably calm, as if a game had come to an end, and for a few moments I was still too, waiting to see what might happen next. But nothing did. Of the five, two were women. All of them had a hard exterior, burnished rough skin, and intense lights to their eyes. I could not read into them whether they were friends or foes, but I looked back at Dina and Darya again, and they were safe, indeed it seemed they were in no danger at all. I was about to say the Turkish guards were coming – urgency came up through me like a flume – but as soon as I opened my mouth, the guards crashed through the door behind me, their rifles raised and all of them shouting orders. But the five did not move. Indeed I was the only one on that roof to cower.

I watched as through the line of guards, their rifles raised, came a commanding officer or some such – a captain – and the rifles lowered. Loquaciously, this officer went up to one of the two women of the five, and they began conversing in Turkish. The woman pointed at Dina and Darya, the officer followed her instruction, and then she did the same to Lou and Stelly. And me? I placed Viktor's revolver carefully on the floor to make clear I was certainly no threat. The officer, it seemed, had something to contemplate, and a phrase kept coming up in Turkish, and the woman pointed at Stelly, and Stelly, his shot-up arm now bound with a rag tourniquet, looked up at them both, as if he was in school detention. He licked his lips and smiled with that ugly reptilian way of his.

The officer rubbed his hand across his chin. It felt as though I was the least of anybody's problems at this moment, so I stepped

144

forward to him. "Sir, you need to understand that these girls are the ones in danger," I said, gesturing to Dina and Darya. He looked at me as if he had not even noticed I was there. "*This* woman is trying to kill them, and she has already killed two men downstairs in one of the rooms."

The look he gave me was almost one of surprise that I was even talking to him at all. And then I realised I had made the mistake of thinking he was the law here, that I was inviting myself into a police procedure, that I was pleading with a court officer.

"This woman?" he said pointing down at Lou. "Trying to kill these girls?"

Lou glared at me.

"Is this true?" the captain said to her.

"He has no idea what he's talking about," she said.

He looked back at me. "She disagrees with you," he said.

He then bent down to Lou and spoke to her in a hushed tone in a language I couldn't place. He looked over to me, as did Lou, and he stroked his chin some more and nodded.

Stelly leaned across to the captain's side and said, "You going to trust her, cap? You going to listen to her? She not from here. She not one of us, cap."

The captain ignored him, and reached behind Lou and cut the binding at her wrists.

"This is a mistake," I said. "She is here to kill these girls."

Dina and Darya waited, clinging to each other.

Lou stood. "I'm here to take them home," she said to me with a stern, angry glare.

The five militia by this point were bystanders, relaxed, leaning: a Francis Benthem-sketch-in-waiting. But when the captain took his revolver from its holster and turned to Stelly, the woman who had been his point of contact stepped forward urgently.

"No," she said. "He is a Golden Orphan." That Turkish phrase again.

145

Stelly grinned and seemed to tense and stretch so his legs pulled out and the veins in his neck pushed from under his woody skin.

"I know who he is," the captain said, and he fired a single shot through Stelly's eye. "And I am not a superstitious Greek."

Dina and Darya convulsed at the scene and I went to them and turned them away.

"And him?" the captain said, and I turned to see he was asking Lou what was to be done with *me*. The five militia were now on edge. The Turks had violated something with the execution of Stelly.

Lou took a moment before saying, "He really doesn't have a clue about anything."

"He can identify you."

"But he won't," Lou said.

The captain holstered his pistol and they both turned away from me as if to discuss more important business.

"I do know one thing," I said. They turned back to me. "I know that nobody needed to die here today. I know that given the choice you chose to do wrong."

Again the captain's expression was one of surprise that I was talking. Lou, however, looked gentle, she looked sympathetic. "You've been here, what, a week? Two?" she said. "In that time did you find out how much those two young girls are worth? I mean how much they are worth in pounds and pence. Evgeny knew. Viktor knew. Christ, they probably know themselves. The people I work for, they have no interest in money. They only care about the status quo. And now they have what they want."

"And Stelly?"

"You don't want to get in the middle of all the people who wanted these girls," Lou said. "Power draws out some unlikely players. And these girls are heirs to a fucking fortune. All they have to do is grow up. Stelly was the one at the house that night.

Who knows who was paying him, or what his instructions were. But a creature like him: they don't tend to have large repertoires."

She gestured to Dina and Darya and they walked to her without any hesitation.

I felt hollow, but I managed to say, "The man I work for is looking for his son."

Lou looked down at the lifeless body of Stelly. "If it *was* him, I have done Illie Prostakov a favour, trust me."

And then she put a consoling arm around the girls. She spoke to them in Russian, in a tone of such warmth and tenderness both girls began to nod and weep and make gestures of thanks. The three of them embraced.

I looked at the five militia who were still unsure of themselves after the execution of Stelly – they were fidgeting and restless. The captain looked around the rooftop, nodded some kind of approval that everything was settled, and touched the peak of his cap to the five. All he had for me was a blank glance as he led his men back through the stairwell door. Lou, with Dina and Darya huddled up to her arms, followed them.

"See you around," she said as she passed me.

Twenty

It was the six of us left on the rooftop, the two sides wondering
what was to happen next. And so I said to the leader of the group,
with a somewhat dejected tone, half-expecting them to shoot me
coldly up there at any moment, "I know a man who is looking
for you."

"There is always somebody looking for us," the woman said.

"But this is different," I said. A plan was emerging in my head,
a plan that had at its centre the mission of keeping me alive as
long as it took to get out of Famagusta.

"How is it different?" she went on. "We are trophies to some
people. Ghosts to others. What use is it to us to be captured?"

"Are you going to shoot me?" I said.

"We do not decide these things," said the woman. "You come
with us now."

They led me at gunpoint down from the roof and out of the
hotel, out into the street. We walked off the main road, and
through a decayed residential area, and then they pointed at me
to go down some steps into what once would have been a square
with a central fountain and gardens, and then across this to the
edges of a small park. Immediately I could see that this was a
basecamp of some sort. Just inside the park were green canvas
tents and evidence of a working space. As we walked, I could see
that what had once been the park had overgrown and spilled out
to lead up to a large building – a municipal building perhaps, with
wide stone steps to a rotating door. But we weren't going to the
municipal building, and I was led off to the left and into still more

overgrowth – it was becoming jungle-like. I couldn't ignore the feeling I was being led to a secluded spot to meet my end.

"Where are you taking me?"

But there was no answer other than a push in the back and a grunt.

I asked again.

"To speak to a man you know," said one of them.

My god, I thought. It came to me like a blow to the head. Francis Benthem was here.

We stopped. The silence fell warmly around us. One of the five went off, and we were just waiting then for him to return. I was waiting for Francis to come out from the thicket. Anywhere other than this place and the very idea would have been absurd – but this was not a world or even a life I recognised. Even the silence of the world was different here, so why could a man not raise from the dead?

And as I was contemplating this absurdity, rubbing my eyes and awaiting the sight of the man I had come here to bury, I saw a break in the trees and bushes.

The light changed. It was as if it was a gateway to a room made of shrubbery and branches. I found myself stepping toward it. I pushed back the edges of the gateway with my hand and there it was. In the thick purple silver light was a red child's swing. It was exactly how I had imagined it in my mind.

There was movement behind me. The woman had returned, and with her was not Francis Benthem as my addled mind had allowed me for a moment to think. No. It was Furkan Balaban. And, my god, if it didn't all come to something then. The municipal building behind us was the hospital. It even looked like a hospital now. The hospital Furkan had been born in, and been left in by his parents when the Turkish invaded.

I could not move or speak. There was too much going through my mind.

Furkan acknowledged me, and then spoke to the leader of the five in Greek. He was being briefed, it seemed. He came to me.

"You have had a difficult day," he said, and offered me a cigarette.

"I wouldn't argue with that," I said. "This isn't one last smoke, is it?"

"You're not in any trouble," he said to my relief.

He stood close to me, his words hushed, and I looked deeply into the glass of his eyes. I could see something there, something in the brilliant Picasso blue of them, and I knew who he was. I did not know what to say.

That his father was a mad Russian – that I could take him to him?

That his mother… I could not bring myself to even think of it.

I wanted to stay silent. I wanted this all to be too much to be correct, but there was no other explanation.

And then I said, "I know where your father is, Furkan."

"What did you say?"

"He has employed me to help him look for you. I did not know at first. But here, now, I know it to be true."

Furkan's demeanour changed, as if his flesh had turned to rock.

"My father, you say?"

Something made me put my hand on Furkan's shoulder in an attempt at some kind of support for him, and he did not flinch at it. He was softening, and then to my surprise he reciprocated the gesture, and he put his hand on my shoulder.

"I knew this was coming," he said. "I have felt something recently. Being here, looking after my people – I have felt something coming. A quiver in my blood."

"I can take you to him," I said, and he looked up at me with a jolt.

"Of course, right, it is the Russian you work for?"

I nodded. He was tearful, and rubbed his eyes clear and wiped his nose on his sleeve. He even took a few deep breaths. I could not think of Tara, could not speak of her. The horror of all that was a dense silence to me as I stood locked with this man. I just looked at Furkan, and saw in him my safe passage out of Famagusta.

Twenty-One

The two of us, with Furkan driving, set off out of Famagusta and toward the house.

When we got there the place was deserted and Furkan began to show the first signs of frustration and a lack of coolness, stomping around the house and waving his arms.

"Wait," I said to him. "He will be down in the woods."

We headed round to the ridge, and there was Tara's car, empty with the driver's door ajar. Furkan looked confused. There was an anger bubbling up inside him. He glared at me.

"I have no idea," I said.

He went off ahead of me toward the wood, down the shale track. I ran to catch up and led Furkan into the woods. He looked in bemusement at the canvases nailed to the trees.

"What is all this?" he said. "What place have you brought me to?"

Whether he recognised the swing in the paintings as the swing from the hospital grounds I could not be certain – he did not mention anything – but his confusion and distress grew and grew.

And then shortly we came upon the small clearing.

Illie was sitting motionless in his chair, and showed no signs of surprise at our appearance. His eyes were red and his face was an ashen pale. There had been something going on here, but now he seemed almost serene.

"I demand to know what is going on here," Furkan bellowed.

I tried to calm him, put a gentle hand to his shoulder, but now it was as if he and Illie were the only people in a vast universe.

Illie did not change his demeanour at all.

He said to me, past Furkan, "You brought him to me."

He turned his attention to Furkan and gestured to the paintings all around.

"When I came to get your mother from the hospital, I could not find her, and eventually I saw her through the window of the ward, and there she was, sitting lonely on that red swing in the park. I came down and took her. She did not want to go. She did not want to leave you. I dragged her from that swing and she screamed and cried. And it swung there with her shape still in it."

Furkan changed at this.

"You *are* my father?" he said softly.

Illie nodded once.

Furkan now strengthened his pose, wiped his face with the palm of his hand, paced a little, glared at the floor, at the paintings, at me.

And then he turned back to Illie. "And my mother?"

It knocked me back. Illie too had a lurch at that. How could he say what Tara had done?

"You have known her," Illie said.

Furkan looked confused. Somewhere in the darkest depths of his mind a dungeon door was opening and the truth was stepping into the light.

"She has walked into the woods," Illie said, gesturing with a slight turn of the head over his shoulder into the darkness beyond the paintings. "You must forgive her everything she has done."

Furkan's face began to twist and crumble. He went off into the woods, a primal scream inches from his lips.

I had been rooted to the spot, but now I turned to Illie. Before I could say anything he looked up at me from his chair and he said, "I think it is time for you to go. There is nothing good to come from all this. We are at the end of a terrible road."

153

I wanted to ask him questions. But I think I knew all the answers.

And so I left.

*

I did not leave Cyprus straight away. Something felt cleared out about Napa, as if it was just going on regardless, which of course it was, and I needed to do the same. I booked into a hotel overlooking Nissi Beach and lived off room service for a week, just watching the holidaymakers do their thing from my balcony. And nothing happened. Nothing changed.

After that week I ventured out. Tara's gallery was closed. Furkan's bars too. I took a scooter up to Paralimni and his bar was closed there as well. I stood in the square and noticed crossing the road that priest who had buried Francis. I waved at him, and he waved back although his face suggested he had no idea who I was. But he approached me, and then something seemed to click and he said, "You decided to stay?" I nodded and then pointed at the bar. "Have you seen Furkan Balaban at all?"

The priest seemed to shake his head, but was non-committal.

"Do you know his partner, Tara?"

The priest just squinted at me.

We stood in silence for a moment, just looking at each other, and then I said, "Well, good to see you."

The priest smiled meekly and patted me gently on the shoulder. He was about to walk off and I said, "Have you any news on Mr Prostakov? You remember the Russian who paid for Mr Benthem's burial?"

"Ah yes," said the priest, and shuffled off back across the square. He called as he went, "My advice would be to just forget it. It's Cyprus." And he shrugged at me again and walked away, with his little hunch and his vacant eyes.

I rode the moped the long journey out to Illie's house. The cars were gone from the garage, the paintings had been taken down from the trees, and so I bagged up my things that were in the tower, leaving the booze and all the paraphernalia. I guess I could have stayed there, but at that point I was just keeping moving. Walking back to the moped along the ridge and past the house I saw through the window that the furniture was gone, all apart from one table in the room where Illie had kept his bar. The kitchen side door was open and so I went in, and as I thought I had seen, there was an envelope on that table. It had my name on it, and in it was ten thousand Euros in cash. No note. I thought about what to do with it. Was it misery money, tainted by what had gone on here? I took it anyway. Misery had to mean something.

It was a few more days before I called Clare. She had been worried about me, but it was a different kind of concern. She did not want to be responsible for me any more – I could hear it in her voice. I said to her that I felt different, that I would like to come home. She said that it was good that I was feeling that way, but she didn't want to give anything between the two of us another go. She was right, of course. She said that when I was back in London we should get together and clear the air, but that she had no ill feelings toward me. She said I should look at this as she had done, as an opportunity for a clean slate. Don't allow the past to swallow you up, she said to me, and I could hear down the line that she said it with an affectionate smile.

Acknowledgements

To Richard Davies for the impetus; to Amelia for the painting of dreams; and to Cyprus for filling in the gaps.